Love

OF A LIFETIME

E. MICHELLE

For permission requests, write to the publisher, addressed "Attention: Permissions Coordinator," 205 N. Michigan Avenue, Suite #810, Chicago, IL 60601. 13th & Joan books may be purchased for educational, business or sales promotional use. For information, please email the Sales Department at sales@13thandjoan.com.

Printed in the U. S. A.

First Printing, October 2024.

Library of Congress Cataloging-in-Publication Data has been applied for.

ISBN: 978-1-961863-14-9

I would like to thank God for giving me a passion for writing. I would like to thank my sister, Wylza, and one of my best friends, Shirley, for reading my manuscript and giving me feedback throughout the years because this book has been in the making for a long time. I want to thank my family, sister circle, and anyone I have encountered that offered me encouragement and their support throughout the years. I would also like to thank anyone who is reading this and can identify with this story.

Growing up, reading was one of my favorite hobbies. I loved reading. I remember reading Sister Souljah's book, *"The Coldest Winter Ever"* and thinking about all the American girls with Caribbean roots, like myself, who I never saw stories about.

This book is for all the girls who grew up as first generation Americans born to Caribbean immigrant parents and living a life grounded in our culture while being "American."

TABLE OF

Contents

THE BIG DAY

Dominique

THE FIRST SATURDAY *of June marked many first experiences in Dominique's life. It was supposed to be the happiest day of her life. In some ways it was, but it was not the way that she always dreamed it to be.*

My name is Dominique Mathieu, I am twenty-six years old, I work as a financial consultant for a major firm, and in a few hours I will be married to a man that loves me very much and would do anything to make me happy. When I was a young girl, I always thought that I would marry the man who was the love of my life, but that was not meant to be. Instead, I am with a man that truly loves me and that I love and care deeply about. I will respect my vows to him by honoring and cherishing him, loving him in sickness and health, and for richer or poorer, but I don't know if my heart will ever be fully his to have. That is not the problem, my husband-to-be knows that he is not the love of my life, however, since he loves me that much, he is willing to do whatever it takes to keep me in his life forever and win my heart completely.

Some of you are probably wondering, why he would do that, or thinking that I must be out of my mind marrying somebody that is not the love of my life. I do love him, and admire him because he does make me happy, he just wasn't the man to light my fire, the man that I thought I couldn't live without, or the man that I would have done anything for. His name is David Baptiste, he is a thirty-year-old lawyer, at a very prestigious law firm. We have been dating now for four years, and since he made me happy, and I knew I didn't want to be alone for the rest of my life, I thought it was about that time to settle down and get married. If it were up to him, we would have been married already, I on the other hand wanted to wait and see if I could truly live with the man that did not fully have my heart. Marrying him was the best decision for me. How many times in my lifetime would I find a handsome successful man, who loved me with all he had, and was willing to do anything for me, knowing that he didn't have my heart fully.

I will tell you up front, I am an independent woman, but I am also realistic. Being alone until I found what I perceived to be the right one was no longer an option for me because you only have the love of your life once and I already had mine, so I knew it wouldn't happen again. I always felt that the older a woman gets and is still unattached, the harder it becomes for her to get married because her options get narrower and narrower, and half of the time she ends up settling anyway. Settling is probably not the right word because I didn't settle with David. David was by far the best choice I made in choosing a life partner. This is not an excuse, this is simply how strongly I feel about marrying someone, building a family and not living alone wondering what could have been if I had done things differently. Maybe my thinking had something to do with my West-Indian parents who instilled in me from day one that one of my major goals in life after getting an education was to get married and have a family.

It was a beautiful Saturday afternoon, the sun was shining, and I was sitting there getting ready to take a trip down the aisle in a few hours. My wedding was set for five in the afternoon at the Lake Shore Manor. Lake Shore Manor was an exquisite hall that housed both outdoor and indoor weddings. The outdoor weddings were held in a breathtaking garden with a gazebo overlooking the lake. I was blessed it was a sunny day, so we didn't have to move the wedding indoors. I was seated in the changing room while getting my make-up done, and other people were running about looking for their items to get ready. Getting here was one of the hardest journeys of my life. I thought about all the pain I went through as a young adult, and had to stop myself from crying as I thought back on things in my life that brought back happy and sad memories. I thought back to when I first met David, and automatically that took my mind back to Kenneth and the heartache that he caused me. My makeup was done, and my makeup artist really outdid herself.

I took a peek into the mirror, and I liked what I saw. In a few more hours I would be married. I took a lot of steps to make sure that this day would turn out perfectly if that were possible. I wanted to remember this day because I only planned on getting married once. As I sat there I thought back to all the experiences in my life that brought me to this present day.

MY BEST FRIEND'S WEDDING

Joanne

IT WAS THE *first Saturday of June, and I was smiling as I was about to serve as my best friend Dominique's Maid of Honor. I thought about the journey it took for her to get here, and that caused me to have a quick flashback to the heartache we both endured before reaching this major milestone.*

My name is Joanne Printemps, I am twenty-six years old, and I am a nurse at a NYC hospital. Today my best friend Dominique is getting married, and Dominique and I go way back. We lived in the same neighborhood, and our parents are good friends. As I am gathering my things to leave and head to the wedding to help Dominique prepare for her big day, there are many thoughts of our friendship going through my mind. I am happy for Dominique because no one deserves to be happier. At the same time, I must admit that I am a little envious of her. I am a little jealous that she is the one walking down the aisle instead of me. I think back on past relationships and lost loves, and I wonder if I should have done anything differently. The thoughts of jealousy ease up as I think about all the things that I have gone through with Dominique always there by my side.

The first boyfriend I had was in the eighth grade, and he was the cousin of Dominique's boyfriend at the time. He was cute, and a little older than me. I didn't like talking to boys my age, so when I saw his interest in me, it was perfect. Getting guys to notice me was never a problem. I was tall, light skin, with long hair. I was nicely developed, and always dressed with the latest trends. Our relationship consisted of going to his house after school, and chilling. Most of the time we would watch videos or listen to music. We were not having sex, but I think he wanted to make his cousin think we were. When I hung out with him, we were always upstairs in his room. I didn't really care because I knew the truth and so did he. We would kiss and feel each other up and that was the extent of our young relationship. I was waiting for that special someone to have sex. Thinking back to my first boyfriend, sometimes it just felt like we were just good friends. I liked him, but I was still waiting for someone better to come along. I wanted someone who excited me. After our 8th grade graduation, we lost touch and Dominique and his cousin broke up that summer. I was looking forward to my freshman year of high school and seeing all the cute and older upper-class boys.

Thinking back to my high school days brought back a lot of fun memories. High school was a lot of fun for me. My freshman year I dated a senior for about a year, but by my sophomore year I was dating another senior. He was really popular and a lot of girls liked him as well, he only talked to the prettiest girls, so us getting together was just a matter of time, but I didn't know that I was not the only one. One day, while walking through the lunchroom on my way to the bathroom, the sixth period lunchroom crowd was in there, and there I saw a girl sitting on his lap and his hand was up her skirt. He didn't see me because he was too involved in what he was doing. She looked at me and gave me a wicked smile like she knew a secret I didn't. I thought about stepping to him, but I didn't want to cause a scene. After school, he waited for me in the usual spot as if everything was cool. I walked up to him, and told him that I didn't want to be with him anymore, all he had to say was that we made the perfect couple.

3

TEENAGE YEARS

Dominique

HE FIRST TIME I was hurt was when I was fourteen. My Haitian parents who were fairly strict warned me about sex. By the time they started talking to me about sex, it was already too late. I became sexually active at the age of thirteen. I was in my last year of junior high school, and I had been with the same boy all year during the eighth grade. He was in all my classes except home economics. I noticed him the first day of class because we were seated in alphabetical order and we ended up sitting right next to each other. He was tall for a thirteen-year-old, and he was dark skin with curly hair. He had a nice smooth complexion. We ended up sitting together in most of our classes because all the teachers seated us alphabetically. I wanted to make a move on him before he showed interest in anyone else, so I suggested we go to class together and exchange numbers in case one of us were ever absent we could get the homework assignment. The first week of school came and went, and he and I hung out a lot and we would sit together during lunch, and walk home together after school. I found out that there were a few girls who were interested in him in my class, but whenever they would ask him if he had a girlfriend he would say yes.

One day in October, when I came back from class I found a note on my desk from him asking me if I wanted to be his girlfriend. We would sneak behind staircases to meet and kiss, until the dean almost caught us one day. It was like the fourth time we had gotten a pass from computer class to go behind our usual staircase to make out. We were really getting into it when we heard voices. He ran down the staircase and I proceeded up the staircase. The dean stopped me, and asked to see my pass I showed it to her and she said your pass is about to expire and told me to get back to class. She asked if there was anyone else in the hallway. I quickly said no and hurried back to class, glad I didn't get caught with him in the staircase which would have meant a phone call home. We cooled down with the passes after that, so we would mostly just kiss and stuff after school.

On another occassion, we were at his cousin's house. My best friend Joanne was with me because she was going out with his cousin. They were in the living room, and we were upstairs in his cousin's room. We were kissing, and then he started to take my clothes off, and he took his clothes off. He kissed my breast, and when he got hard, he stuck it in. It hurt a little at first, and before I had a chance to like it, he was done. I started to lose interest in him, and when school let out in the summer I didn't really stay in touch with him, especially since we were going to different high schools anyway.

I was a freshman in high school, and on my first day of school I saw the guy who became my crush. He was a senior on the basketball team, and he had the juiciest lips ever. I bumped into him in the hallway a lot. I was walking with a friend of mine and we crossed paths with him and he said hello to my friend first and then to me since I was with her. From that day on, whenever I saw him in the hallway, he would say hi. The last week of September, I was in the library looking for a book. He came up behind me and said, "your name is Dominique, right?" He introduced himself officially and we started talking. He asked if he could wait for me until I was done. Since we couldn't talk in the library, we went outside. We were both on a free period. We talked about him wanting to get a basketball scholarship to Virginia State for college and my life as a freshman. He asked me if I had a boyfriend or had interest in anyone. I told him I was interested in him, and he said he was interested in me too. He gave me his number and asked me to call him that night. He walked me to my class, and told me he would wait for me after school. After school, we rode the train home together.

I called him that night, and we talked for about an hour. We started to meet at the train station in the morning, so we could ride to school together. His best friend, Joanne, my other best friend Stacey, and I would all meet and ride the train to school together. We all went home together in the afternoon. Thinking back, he never really asked me out, I guess it was just understood that we were together. He was really sweet, for our first month together, he bought me a teddy bear. Joanne would wait with me when I waited for him after basketball practice. Since his friend was also on the basketball team and the four of us hung out, they eventually got together. It was cool because we would all hang out together.

In our third month together, we cut school and went to his house. As a gift, he bought me a chain with a heart pendant with our initials. I bought him a Michael Jordan jersey, since that was his favorite player. We watched music videos, listened to music, and played video games. After a while, we went into his room and we started kissing. We kissed for a while, then he undressed me and started to finger me for a long time. He asked me if he could put it in. He was a nice size, and he knew what he was doing, so I actually had a chance to enjoy this experience. He was not a virgin, and I was glad he had experience. Since my first experiment with sex had not been pleasurable, I was glad that I liked sex with him and it seemed like he wanted me to enjoy the experience as well. I still had a lot of questions about sex, but I didn't know whom to ask. Afterwards, he was smiling from ear to ear. I went to Mr. Varsity's house a lot after school. Once inside his room, we would get right to it, and each time felt better and better. I couldn't understand why my parents said I should wait until marriage to have sex. I didn't want to have to wait that long to have this feeling. Later, I would learn I should have taken my parents' advice, or at least wait until I was more mature to begin having sex because I didn't realize what a huge responsibility sex was.

We had a lot of fun together, he was the ideal boyfriend. I really liked him, and I knew he really liked me. As the months whizzed by, I started to think about the fact that he would be leaving in July to go away to school. Although school would start in August, he planned on attending a basketball camp for three weeks before school started. I tried not to think about it. The senior prom was in early June, and he paid for our prom tickets. The prom was held at a hotel and we had lots of fun and danced all night. Graduation had arrived and I took lots of pictures and was so proud of him, but I realized how much I would miss him as well as he embarked on the next chapter. After the ceremony, I went out with his family to eat and we had a good time. I went back to his house afterwards and we just hung out. We were trying to squeeze in as much time together because he was leaving soon.

Although he would be leaving in a month, Mr. Varsity never talked about breaking up or staying together. One night, about a week before he left, we were hanging in his room, and he explained he wanted us to stay together while he went away to college. He said he would try to call me as much as he could, and write to me, and we would see each other when he came down during breaks. I didn't know how I felt about a long-distance relationship because I was young and not ready to think about something so serious, but because I really liked him, I agreed. He was my first real boy-friend. I had boyfriends in junior high school, but it wasn't the same. I did a lot with him, and he gave me things. We just had a lot of fun together, and I couldn't imagine that another guy would do all the things we did. The night before he left, we had sex for the last time, and I cried when I left his house because I knew how much I would miss him. He called me in the morning before he left. That was the last time I ever heard from him. I didn't know exactly when he planned on coming back from his camp, but he never called me. When I called him in August, his sister told me that he had already left for school. For the rest of the summer, I waited in the house all day for him to call me, but he never did. I don't even know what happened. That was my first heartbreak, and my first experience of getting cut off without any explanation or closure. If only someone had warned me that this would not be my last, maybe I would have sworn off men altogether. The rest of the guys I talked to just made me realize that most men are not truthful about most things in the beginning, and they each con-tributed in taking pieces of me that I would never fully get back.

When I went back to school in September, it was kind of strange because I hung out with Mr. Varsity so much that it felt weird not doing that anymore. Going back to school made me realize it was definitely time to move on. In my biology class was this boy who was popular in school that I thought was cute. I wasn't sure if he was a sophomore or junior. In lab class, we were divided into groups of four. Luckily, I ended up in his group. To be safe we all exchanged numbers. After class he and I were walking in the same direction and I struck up a conversation by asking him if he was a sophomore or junior. He told me he was a junior and immediately asked if me and him were still together. I simply told him we had broken up over the summer without reliving my heartbreak or the feeling of getting played. Things were beginning to look up. Maybe the school year would not be so bad after all.

He and I started dating, but it didn't last long because he started acting possessive. He would try and tell me what to wear. He would call me at home really late to make sure I was home, and my parents were not trying to hear that. He didn't give me any breathing room. When I was chilling with Joanne or Stacey he would act up. I broke up with him in December. Over the Christmas vacation he called me a lot, but I didn't want to speak to him. When I went back to school, he came by my classes, and I ignored him, so he finally got the picture and left me alone.

I decided I would take a break from the guys in the school. There was this guy that had just moved around my neighborhood that I had my eye on. One day, I was coming from Joanne's house, and as I turned the corner, he was coming out of his house. He stopped me and asked me for my name. I gave him the info, and although I looked older than my age, I never lied about it. He said I was young, but that he thought I seemed mature, so he gave me his number. He told me to call him that night. I didn't believe in waiting to call anyone, so I did as he asked, and called him. We spoke for a bit, and he told me he had just moved to NYC from Florida. I asked him if he liked it so far, and he said Florida was too slow paced for him. Going out with him was cool because he would come and pick me up from school, and of course I couldn't leave my friends behind, and he didn't seem to mind giving them rides home. Since he was older, he also put pressure on me to have sex with him. Sex with him was ok, but he didn't take the time out to really satisfy me, after he got his that was it. What was funny is that he really thought he was doing something special. Most of the times when we did it, I would just let my mind wander and think about other things, until he was done which was usually not that long. I began to notice things about him that I was scared to admit to myself.

When I asked him if he worked, he said he was looking for a job, yet he always had money in his pockets, he maintained his car, and had the nicest gear. A lot of things didn't add up, until I started to hear rumors around the block that he was a drug dealer. Messing with a drug dealer was not an option for me, so I had to cut him off. He couldn't understand why I wanted to cut him off, and said if I didn't want to talk to him, he better not see me with another guy either, and he would be watching me. What was wrong with these men acting possessive, as if I was their property. He would still come by my school to pick me up. I would refuse the ride, and keep it moving with my friends. There were a lot of girls sweating him, and I heard that he would have sex with them, but he wasn't trying to start a relationship. I just wanted him to leave me alone.

One afternoon, on my way home from school, he cornered me and I got really scared because he wouldn't let me go. I finally gave in and went to his house like he asked me too. He said he just wanted to talk. Inside his house, he asked me why I suddenly broke up with him. He thought I was happy with him, and that he treated me right. There wasn't anything wrong with the way he treated me, it was just that he was dealing drugs, and I was not trying to get caught up with that. I wasn't about to tell him that cause then he would want to know where I heard it from. I didn't want to get involved in dropping dimes on anyone. When I didn't answer he tried to kiss me, and I pushed him away. That made him angry, and then he pushed me on the bed and got on top of me. I looked him dead in the eye and said this is why I don't want to be with you. You are too forceful and possessive. He backed off of me and apologized. He said he really liked me, and that he was going to make sure he got me back. Even though I didn't live far from him, he insisted on taking me home. I told him I was going to Joanne's house, so he dropped me there.

I told Joanne what happened when I got to her house, and she said, maybe I should just tell him the truth. I thought about that, but the more I thought about his temper, I didn't think it was a good idea. The only thing that I was looking forward to at this point was the fact that school would be ending. I was also secretly hoping that Mr. Varsity would be back in the summer and maybe he would call me or come by. Unfortunately, my neighborhood ex kept bothering me, and when I didn't know what else to do, I got back with him, but I told him I didn't want him picking me up because somebody had seen me in his car and told my parents, and they would be watching me more closely. Whenever he asked me to come over, I would just make an excuse as to why I couldn't come, I knew I couldn't keep doing that, but before I got a chance to make any more excuses, he disappeared, and I later found out that he had been locked up.

I missed my ex basketball boo terribly, and decided to call him, but to my surprise the number had been disconnected, and no further information was available. Later, I found out that his family had moved down south. I was crushed all over again. There was no way I would ever talk to him again, unless he decided to contact me. The summer started off dull for me because I was pining about him. I didn't want to go to summer school, and I didn't have to work because my parents gave me whatever I wanted, and if they didn't get it for me my brothers or sisters would get it for me. I had a lot of time on my hands. Having time on my hands is what got me in trouble. I hung out with Joanne and Stacey a lot. We would chill at each other's houses or go out and cruise the malls. We liked going to the malls in the summertime because there were always a lot of cuties there.

It was mid-August when I met my summer fling for that year. I went downtown to meet Joanne because she wanted to get some cheesecake from Junior's. I was waiting for her in the front when he rolled up on me. He stopped and asked me who I was waiting for. I told him I was waiting for a friend. He asked if he could wait with me, so I was like that's up to you because I don't own this street. I wasn't really in the mood to talk to anyone. I was hoping Joanne would hurry up. He started telling me that he went to summer school at Long Island University which was across the street from Juniors. He told me that he would be a sophomore in September, and that he would be nineteen in November. I didn't really give him much feedback, I just listened to him talk. He asked me for my number, and when I declined, he asked if he gives me his number, will I call him. I said I don't know you'll just have to wait and see. He gave me his number, and waited with me until Joanne came then I introduced them and he left. I started to throw his number away, but I put it in my pocket instead, I later would have wished that I threw the number away.

I called him like a week later, and this time I didn't give him such a hard time, and I found that our conversation was cool. He seemed like a really cool guy. He went to school full time and worked part time at the Gap. At least, he had a job that I knew about. Things started off slowly with him because he said he wanted to take his time with me. School started before I knew it, and on his days off from work, he would come pick me up and ride the train with us. Sometimes, I would go to his house, he lived in Flatbush, and we would watch videos and just chill. We kissed and stuff, but he never took it further. We were together for seven months before we had sex, and soon after that some girl called my house questioning me about him. She said she was his girlfriend and I better stop messing with her man. I told him about it and he said it was just his ex-girlfriend trying to get back with him. I asked him how she got my number if she was just his ex, and he gave me a story that seemed believable.

I didn't break up with him, and the girl kept calling my house. I decided to set up a three-way, to hear what he would have to say. The girl called him and started questioning him about me. I heard him say that I was just some junior in high school that was sweating him, and he had been trying to let me down easy, but I just wouldn't give up even though he told me he had a girlfriend. He admitted to her that we slept together only once which was a lie, and that he wanted to be with her because he only liked me, but was in love with her. I guess that was enough for her because she told him the truth about the three-way. He cursed her out. I hung up, and when he called me later to explain, I didn't want to hear his lies, and hung up on him. As a gift that year, my parents gave me my own phone line in my room, and it came at a good time. He kept calling me for like a week, but I just kept hanging up on him. Eventually, he stopped. I don't think he really cared anyway since he was probably still with that girl. Of course, I got my answer when she called me back to tell me she would appreciate it if I didn't call her man anymore. I told her I didn't want him, so she could have him all for herself.

MY INNOCENCE IS GONE

Joanne

T WAS THE summer before my senior year in high school when life changed in more ways than one. My parents usually went on vacation to Florida for the summer, and sometimes I stayed behind. This summer I chose to go, and my best friend Dominique was able to go with us. We spent most days at the beach, but things got really interesting on our third day at the beach. I was still a virgin because my Haitian parents drilled waiting until marriage in my head since I could remember.

Meeting Bernard certainly changed a lot of things in my life. Bernard was cute, and the moment we met, our attraction was mutual. I was drawn to Bernard instantly. I never felt that strongly about anyone I went out with. He had a body to die for, and he was fine. When we started talking on the beach, we had a lot to talk about. I decided then and there that this was the person I had been waiting for. I couldn't believe how crazy this was. I mean I had talked to guys before, and the idea of losing my virginity to any of them never crossed my mind, and then suddenly this handsome stranger came along, and I knew in that moment, he was the one.

We sat on the beach and he told me about himself. Bernard was twenty-four, and he was a real estate broker. The more he spoke, the more I felt myself melting under his charm. Bernard made me want to do things that I had never really thought about before. At that moment, I felt like I wanted to kiss him. I don't know how I managed to hold back all the things I was feeling. Dominique and his friend seemed to be hitting it off, so when he suggested that we all go out later that evening, I was more than willing. We gave them our address and phone number and left. Once in the car, I told Dominique that he was the one, which shocked her. Dominique knew that I wanted to wait for that special someone, so the bomb I dropped was heavy. She asked me if I was sure since I had waited so long. I explained the connection that I felt towards Bernard, and how my stomach was in knots, and I was a little nervous, but I knew he was it. When we reached home, we were both excited about going out that evening. I took out so many different outfits before I finally decided on one. I decided to go with a long black skirt with thigh high splits, a black lacy bra, and sheer top. Dominique gave me some condoms and told me to be careful.

We went to an Italian restaurant, and the food was delicious and the conversation flowed throughout the evening. That night everything seemed extra tasty. Although dinner was going well, I felt a little anxious because I couldn't wait to be alone with Bernard. Dominique and his friend, Wes, went to a club, and as I sat in Bernard's car, I built up enough courage to reach over and kiss him. Kissing Bernard set off all types of alarms, and my body reacted in so many ways. I felt the heat coming from between my thighs and couldn't wait to take the big step with him.

After that kiss, no other words were needed and we drove off in silence. I couldn't believe that this total stranger had me completely mesmerized and had taken my breath away. I was in deep thought, and didn't notice when the car stopped moving. He came around to open my door, and got me out of my trance. He escorted me out, and held me and kissed me, and once again it felt like I was floating. He opened the trunk and took out the blankets from that afternoon, and that's when I noticed that we were back at the same beach that we had been at earlier that day. He led me to the sand. We walked towards the water, and he found a secluded spot. We sat down, and he started kissing on my ears and neck. My body felt things that I never felt before.

He took my shirt off, and slid my bra off. He licked each nipple, and then took his time on each breast. Then he scooted on top of me, and I could feel his hardness. He took his pants off and came out of his boxers, and I reached over to my bag and grabbed a condom. He smiled, rolled it on, and slid inside me. It was a little uncomfortable at first. He noticed and took it slowly. He slowly stroked inside me and when it started to feel good, I started moving with him to match his pace. I didn't know what I was doing, but it felt right. He stroked for a while, and when he quickened his pace, I knew this was the moment, my heartbeat quickened as I moved with him, and then we exploded. He collapsed on top of me. I heard a voice say I love you, and I realized it was me, when he said I love you too. We put our clothes back on, and sat there.

He asked, "was this your first time?"

"Yes." Before he could say anything else I told him the moment I met him, I knew that he was the special someone I had been waiting on.

Then he said, "I knew you were that special someone too."

We had to meet Dominique and Wesley back at the house at two, so I figured it was time for us to get a move on. We got to the house with five minutes to spare. While waiting for Dominique, we started kissing again. Before anything else happened, we heard a tap at the window, and it was Dominique. We both laughed. I gave him one last peck on the lips before getting out of the car. I couldn't wait to tell Dominique about the beach. As soon as we were in our room, I told her all the details that went down. We talked into the early morning, and finally fell asleep around six in the morning as the sun was coming up.

I woke up around two that afternoon, and Bernard called around two thirty to make plans for the evening. Bernard and Wesley arrived at nine on the dot, wearing khaki shorts, a polo shirt, and a pair of leather moccasins. He kissed me and then went around to open the door for me. Bernard was the perfect gentleman. He asked me where I wanted to go, and I told him I just wanted to spend time with him. He drove to his place. Once inside, he put some music on and led me to his terrace. The terrace had two patio chairs, and a chaise. I sat on the chair, taking in the view of the (night) sky. It was glistening with stars, kind of romantic. He came back with drinks on a tray. There was a light breeze, and I wanted to enjoy it.

I tried my best to look into his deep brown eyes, "Did you mean it when you said I love you?" I barely whispered.

His face rose in a genuine smile, "I never felt this way about anyone before. It just felt as though we knew each other forever." He made eye contact with me, and I could barely move under his intense gaze. " I just never had such a strong physical reaction to another woman." I felt like we were meant to be, and I know that whatever happened he would be the love of my life. I don't know how I knew that at such an early stage in our relationship, but I knew it was true. We talked about his past relationships, and why he wasn't involved with anybody. He explained that he was just focused on work and wasn't serious with anyone at the moment. We talked for a long time before making our way to his bedroom. I let my eyes wander across every inch of his place. He had a large two-bedroom apartment. His master bathroom was huge with a spa tub and separate shower, and a huge walk-in closet that could have been another bedroom. His living room was furnished with a massive entertainment system. His couch was a deep tan color. His dining room had his equipment. He had bar stools to compliment his extended countertops. The second bedroom was used as an office. He had a king-size sleigh bed in his bedroom. We were in the room for less than a minute before he led me to the bed. music was playing softly in the background.

He pulled my tube top over my head and went to work on my breast. He stopped, sliding up to kiss me. His tongue was magic. He sucked on my lips, then sucked on my tongue. He went back down to my breast, then slid down to my belly button. He stuck his middle finger into my wetness, and then did what no one had ever done. He put his tongue inside my wetness, sending chills down my spine. I felt like I was going to explode. I told him to stop because I needed to go to the bathroom. He stopped and said no you don't. I started to get upset. Why was he telling me I didn't need to use the bathroom? When I pushed his head away, and jotted off to the bathroom, I couldn't pee. I wiped myself and realized how wet I was. Bernard asked if I used the bathroom, I said no with a little attitude and felt kind of silly. He laughed and told me I was about to climax. I felt stupid because I missed out on my first orgasm.

I wanted to touch him, and try to make him feel the same way he had made me feel, but I was scared. What if he didn't like what I was doing? He saw the uncertainty in my eyes, and asked me what was wrong. I wasn't about to tell him what thoughts were going through my mind. He pulled me on top of him, and asked me again what was wrong. Instead of answering, I started kissing him, and then started sucking on his neck. He was stroking my back and that encouraged me to continue. I slid down to his chest and licked on his nipples like he did mine. He seemed to enjoy that because his breathing got heavier. I was on my way down, and I was nervous because I had never done this before, but I had come too far to turn back. He noticed my hesitation and said, "you don't have to if you don't want to." I stared at his erect penis for a minute, and lightly licked it at first. I then sucked on the top part just a little bit, and then I just used my imagination, and took it from there. I wasn't sure if I liked it or not, but I liked the reaction I was getting from him. He was pulling on my hair with one hand and rubbing the back of my neck with the other. It felt good, so I just kept going, until I felt it throbbing. Just as I pulled away, he came. He pulled me towards him and started kissing me again, and just held me there on top of him. I laid there and thought about everything that had just taken place. If I didn't know for sure, I knew then that I was in love. Thinking about love was scary. I knew that I was the type of person to love hard and with all my heart. So I just hoped that everything turned out for the best.

I dozed off, and when I woke up it was minutes to three. I inched closer to him to wake him gently, I felt his hardness on my back. Before I could say anything, he got on top of me, and slid inside me. It felt too good to stop, even though we didn't have on a condom. He came inside me, and I felt so connected to him. I figured I should probably go on birth control because I liked the way he felt without the condom. I looked at the time and had to get home. It was four in the morning when I got home, and Dominique was waiting in Wes' car, so we could sneak in together.

Bernard called me later that afternoon to make plans for the evening. He said he would be there to pick me up at about eight and had a surprise for me. I asked him what he had in mind, he said it was a surprise. I asked him what I should wear, and he said something easy to slip off. I decided to wear a short red spaghetti strapped slip-on dress, and I had wrap-around red sandals to go with it. I parted my hair in the middle and curled the ends. I grabbed some toiletries and put them in my bag, and I grabbed a handful of condoms because I wasn't on the pill yet. Now that I was thinking rationally, I knew the last thing I needed was to risk getting pregnant or catching anything. No matter how I felt about him, the fact remained that I did not know him for long.

We went to a posh restaurant, and then an art gallery. I didn't know what to expect, but I enjoyed it since it was different from the things I normally did. We headed back to his place after. We played strip black jack, until all of my clothes were off. He pulled me close to him, and looked me straight in the eyes and said. "Joanne, I want you to know that I love you, and I have waited a long time to meet someone like you." I was wondering where he was going with this. When he said, "I know that we just met, but I want to make you mine. We will have to find a way to work out the distance, but I want to make this official." I never gave long distance relationships much thought. Yet I felt like Bernard was worth it.

I figured I could apply to colleges in Florida and be closer to him. I thought about how much I was falling for him already, and knew it would just get deeper. I kissed him to seal the deal. He laid my head in his lap and just stroked my hair and cheeks. It was about two in the morning when we left his place. We were both quiet as he drove me home, but it was a comfortable silence. He gave me a lingering kiss before I got out of the car, and I went home feeling giddy. My heart was beating quickly and my stom-ach was in knots feeling like I had finally met my dream man. The distance wasn't what I hoped for, but in my mind we could work through anything. That night I fell asleep with a smile on my face. I woke up the next morning to the smell of sausage and eggs. I found Dominique in the kitchen in a surprisingly good mood. I asked her how her date went, and she filled me in on the details. Then I told her about my exciting news, and she said she was happy for me, but asked how we were going to make it work with the distance. I told her I would visit him in the summertime, and apply to schools in Florida.

We went to the movies that night and out to eat afterwards, the evening ended young. I think it was because everyone had a lot of thinking to do. I saw the sparks that were flying between Dominique and Wesley, and I also knew how she wouldn't do a long-distance relationship. I needed time to think about the things I was feeling every time I was around Bernard, and I guess he needed time to let things settle as well. Bernard was the first guy who would light up as soon as he saw me, and I had an identi-cal reaction when I saw him. It's like my insides felt the happiness too, and it was crazy because it happened so quickly. I felt safe and at peace with Bernard. I felt as if he was the key that fit every part of me.

The remainder of the time flew by, we had a lot of double dates with Wesley and Dominique, spent lots of time alone and just had fun, and before we knew it there were just a few days left before

I went back to N.Y. The night before we left, Bernard booked us a room in a hotel. That night with Bernard was passionate and memorable. We did it in the jacuzzi and on the patio. He took his time, kissing me all over my body, and in places I never imagined would bring me pleasure. When he went downtown, I was whimpering like a puppy. This time when I felt like I had to use the bathroom, I let the feeling take over me and came fiercely. I started shaking and knew what it was like to feel immense pleasure. Then I had to return the favor and went downtown on him until he came. He laid there for a few minutes and then told me to turn around so that I was laying on my stomach. He placed some pillows under my chest and told me to stick my butt up in the air. He then slipped it in from the back. I never tried this position before, but it allowed him to go deeper. That night, I tried so many different positions. We laid there in the aftermath of it all and fell asleep. Going home was going to be hard since I couldn't help feeling like I was leaving my heart behind.

5
SUMMER BREAK

Dominique

I WAS LOOKING FORWARD to this summer because my parents were letting me go to Florida with Joanne's family. I was also excited because this was going to be my senior year. Going to Florida was cool because Joanne and I went shopping to get clothes to wear for our new trip. We spent the whole summer in Florida. Her parents had a vacation house out there. There was a huge pool in the backyard, so we sat by the pool or went to the beach. We went to South Beach while we were out there and had a great time. I met a very attractive guy named Wesley. He was cool to hang out with and took us around a few times. Although we were attracted to each other, nothing came of it. I was not interested in a long-distance relationship. We promised to remain in contact with each other. He had a friend, so most of the time the four of us hung out together. Florida was a nice distraction from home, so I was a little sad when we left. Wesley turned out to be a very easy-going guy.

My last night in Florida, I decided I wanted to give him something to remember me by. He rented a hotel, and we had sex. I won't say making love because we didn't feel that way about each other. He was tender and took his time to make me feel good. He was the first guy that went downtown and it drove me crazy. He maneuvered his tongue like a professional. Sex with him was the best so far. He made it seem like everybody before him was insignificant. That was the best night I had in Florida. I went back home with a new energy. I was definitely going to keep in contact with Wesley that way if he ever came to N.Y. or we could hook up if I went to Florida again.

There were only two weeks left before school would start when we got back to N.Y., so of course Joanne, Stacey, and I used that time to go shopping for the latest gear to go back to school. When September rolled around, we were excited because we were seniors.

There was a cutie I had my eye on. We didn't have any classes together, but Joanne told me that she heard that he liked me too. It was the last Friday in September when he finally stepped to me. I was walking with Joanne and Stacey, and he asked if he could talk to me for a minute. He asked me for my phone number and said he would call me that night. He called me that night around eight o'clock. We talked for a while about school, and trivial things before he told me that he liked me. He told me that although he liked me, he didn't want a relationship because he already had a girlfriend. They were in a long-distance relationship because she moved to Pennsylvania when her father's job moved. He said he was hoping that we could accompany each other on the senior activities because his girlfriend would not be able to attend any.

He said after graduation, he was planning on going to college in P.A. to be closer to her. This was a good idea to me because this way I wouldn't have to worry about relationship issues or being hurt again by another guy.

THE END OF SUMMER

Joanne

WHEN WE GOT home there was only two weeks left for school to start. The only thing that made me happy was the fact that it was my last year of high school, and that I would be in Florida soon enough. All I could do was think about Bernard and the wonderful times we spent together. School started and just as I was starting to get into the mix of things, things took a serious turn, my period was seven days late. I called Planned Parenthood to set up an appointment for a pregnancy test, and they said that I had to wait at least fourteen days. Day eight came and there was still no sign of it. I began to panic because I didn't know what I would do if I were pregnant. My parents would be furious, and would probably cut me off, and how would I tell Bernard? Would he be happy? What if he dumped me? I was slowly going crazy as each day passed and still no sign of it. I didn't know if I would have the heart to have an abortion, and I was petrified that something would go wrong. I didn't want to speak to Bernard until I was sure, but I had to share this with someone.

I called Dominique and told her to come over and she was there in less than five minutes. As soon as she closed the door to my room, I started crying and could barely get my words out. She helped me calm down, and let me get my words out. She said she would be there for me whatever I decided to do. Dominique didn't believe in abortions, and said I could move in with her family if it came to that because she knew my parents would flip. On the fourteenth day, Dominique and I went to Planned Parenthood, and the test came back negative, but she told me to come back if I still didn't get my period by the following week. I was relieved, but still a little scared, until my period came three days after that.

I finally called Bernard to tell him what was going on with me. He called during everything and could tell something was wrong, but he would let me tell him when I was ready. I broke down and told him I thought I was pregnant, and how difficult that was for me, especially since he wasn't there to comfort me like I would have wanted him to be. He said I should have told him because even though he wasn't there in person, he would have helped me through it, and supported me with whatever decision I made. He believed that children should always be taken care of, and we could have become a family, if it had come to that. I was relieved to hear him say that, and I told him I was thinking about going on birth control, but I didn't know if it was such a good idea, since we didn't see each other much. He said maybe I should get on it before I came down for the summer, and if we saw each other before that then we would just use protection. It was only

September, and I was already missing him like crazy. I didn't know how I was going to get through the next few months.

The school year was progressing, and I started having fun with the activities that were planned for us. In October, there was a costume party for the seniors, and then in November we had our pajama party. In December, we went on our ski trip, and in February, there was a Valentine's Day dance. It was a little depressing because it made me miss Bernard even more. I almost didn't go, but Dominique and Stacey convinced me to go. In March, I joined the prom committee, so that kept me busy. April was Senior Day, and in May was our trip to Hershey Park. June rolled around with college acceptances, and I was excited when I got into Florida State. Our prom was set for the first Saturday of June at 9 pm.

The Thursday before prom, I got the best surprise of my life. After school, I walked out to find Bernard there with flowers in his hand. I was so excited that I started crying. He wiped my tears and kissed me. Dominique stood there smiling, and I knew she had something to do with this. I clung to him like this was the last time I would see him. I couldn't contain myself, "I missed you so much. How long will you be staying?" He slyly grinned at me, "until your graduation." I was so happy that I didn't know what to say. He asked Dominique to take the flowers home for me because he said he had a surprise for me. She smirked and we parted ways at the train station.

We went to his hotel, where we immediately made up for lost time. Being on the pill was a bonus because I just wanted him to fill me up. Our reunion was better than I imagined. Bernard just surprised me more and more. After we went for a couple of rounds, we went out to eat because we were hungry. At dinner, I told him my good news about being accepted to Florida State. I thought I noticed a look of disappointment on his face, but before I could say anything, he said, "that's great baby." He said he was looking forward to us being together, and he talked about all the things we would do together. He said, "I love you so much, I will do whatever I have to do to keep you. If you keep on being this good to me, and honest with me then I am here to stay." I jokingly said going downtown doesn't hurt either, and we both laughed. That night he came over to my house to meet my parents. They were polite and had small talk with him, and then retired to their room. That was kind of surprising because they would usually wait until my friends left to go to their room. We talked for hours about various things, and I was just happy to have him so close to me. He was in the middle of a sentence when I leaned in to kiss him just because. It was about midnight when he left. I wanted to go with him, but felt comfort in the fact that I would get to see him again for the next few days after that. When I walked him to the door, I gave him a long kiss goodnight. I felt him come alive, and we did it right there in the hallway. It was exciting and terri-fying at the same time because my parents were upstairs. I didn't believe what I had just done, but it was fun. I shoved him out the door before I had any more crazy ideas.

The next day in school, I was so happy, I felt like I was floating. I knew Bernard was meeting me after school again, but I didn't know what he had planned for us. When it hit two forty-five, I rushed out the school doors. I saw the girls in school checking him out, and I felt giddy that he was all mine. I ran up to him and hugged him. It seemed like every time I saw him, I was more excited than the last. I kissed him, and hugged him some more. Dominique said hi to Bernard, and left with Stacey. We went to Coney Island and played games, rode the bumper cars, and a few rides. We had a good time, and Bernard wouldn't quit until he won me a teddy bear. I named the bear Bernie. When it started to get dark, we strolled on the boardwalk and headed for the beach. This beach was nothing compared to the ones in Florida.

We sat on the boardwalk and talked. We both got quiet for a while, each lost in our thoughts. I was thinking at that moment that I would do anything I had to do to keep him in my life forever. I could see myself married to Bernard. I let my mind wander to how beautiful our kids would be, and what I would name them. I was deep in my thoughts when I felt his hand creeping up my thighs. I turned and saw the look in his eyes. He was looking at me so intensely, and it really turned me on. He started nibbling on my ears, and he knew that drove me crazy. When I tried to push him away, he held my hand and sucked on my ears even more. He then started sucking on my neck, and I had to push him away. I didn't want him to give me a hickey on my neck before prom. He found a secluded area and started kissing me deeply. He pushed my panties to the side, and slipped inside me. We were off in a corner, but I couldn't believe it because people could still see us. It was a quickie that would be continued later. I wanted to get home early so that I could have enough time to prepare myself for the next day. I wished he was the one taking me to the prom, but I was going with Dominique's cousin as my date. I never met him before, but I didn't mind because it was just for that night. He dropped me home, but didn't stay long at all.

I woke up early on Saturday. There were a lot of things that needed to be done. I had my dress made, so I had to pick it up at the cleaners. I had to get a manicure, pedicure and my hair done. I did a French roll, with drop curls in the front and some loose tendrils of drop curls coming from the bun. My hair was done around two in the afternoon. I went across the street and started on my pedicure. I got a French pedicure in a peachy color, to match my nails as well. I was done at the nail salon at about five. So I had to rush home to take a shower and begin getting ready. My mom already picked up my dress for me at the cleaners. The limo would arrive by eight. Dominique and I lived so close to each other that we decided to pick her up and take pictures with our dates at her house. At that moment, I felt sad that Bernard wasn't my date.

There was a knock on my door, and when I said, come in, Bernard walked in. I couldn't hug him too close cause I didn't want to mess up my make-up or get it on his clothing. He said he just wanted to see me before my big night, and hoped I had fun, but not too much without him. I put my dress on so that my parents could take some pictures of me before I left. My dress was peach. It was off the shoulders and came out like a gown on the bottom with a bow on the back. The limo stopped at Dominique's and she looked beautiful in her gown. She was wearing a soft pink gown with matching pink gloves. I went in and her parents took pictures of us.

This was going to be the first time that I met my date. Dominique's date walked in alone, looking quite handsome in his tux, but I was wondering where her cousin was. He wore a black tux, with a white shirt, and white bowtie. He presented Dominique with her corsage, and her parents took more pictures. I got the second biggest surprise of that week when Bernard walked in looking quite debonair with his tux on. When did all this happen? Dominique's parents snapped a shot of me to capture the look I had on my face, and then Bernard moved in and they snapped pictures of us, and then of the four of us together. Bernard escorted me to the limo, and I hugged him. I didn't care if I messed up my makeup or not. As soon as the driver started driving, I asked him so many questions at once. When did he plan this? He just smiled and said he had lots of help from Dominique.

I smiled at her knowing she knew how happy I would be. At that moment, I felt so special and loved to have a best friend who would go to great lengths to make me happy, and a thoughtful boyfriend.

Our prom was at the Marriott in midtown Manhattan. As we arrived, there were other limos arriving and dropping off students. Bernard escorted me out of the limo, and there was someone in front of the hotel snapping shots of couples and we proudly got our pictures taken. We waited for Stacey because she was coming with some people who lived closer to her house. She arrived shortly looking lovely with her date on her arms. They stopped to take a picture, and met us by the lobby. When we walked inside there were lots of girls that I barely spoke to that came by to say hi really wanting to get a close-up look of Bernard, so that they could talk about it later. There were a lot of girls wishing that Bernard was their date. If he noticed all the attention he was getting, he didn't let on because he was staring at me. We went to the table and I grabbed a few hors d'oeuvres. I grabbed a drink, and as soon as I had my last sip, Bernard swept me off to the dance floor. The dance floor was tastefully decorated. A slow song was playing, but I don't even remember what it was because I was so enthralled with Bernard. He whispered in my ear that he couldn't wait to get me alone. We danced to a few more slow songs then some upbeat music came on. My feet were hurting, but I still didn't sit down.

Dinner was served, and we ate and talked for a while to let the food settle down. Bernard and I were lost in our own thoughts. I started to feel hot just being so close to him and not being able to touch him. I wondered if he would look that good at our wedding. *Whoa! Where had that thought come from?* I guess that was my heart's desire to be walking down the aisle in a beautiful white dress, and seeing Bernard at the other end of the church. I smiled.

He asked me what that smile was all about, and I told him I was just thinking about him, and how I always wanted him in my life. He smiled, and said he wants the same thing too. We got up to dance, and although Hip Hop was playing we danced slowly to the music.

Sometime after midnight, Bernard led me off the dance floor and we headed towards the elevators. I didn't even ask because he was full of surprises. The elevator stopped on the fifth floor. He slid a key into room #508, and I thought that was cute because that was my birthday backwards. In the room there were two peach roses on the bed with a note attached. Bernard pulled me into a tight embrace that I had been longing for all night. He undid my dress and neatly hung it up, and he undressed and hung his clothes up neatly as well. Then he came towards me, and this time he started kissing my feet, sucked on my toes, and worked his way up. I was thankful for pretty feet, and a nice pedicure.

He paused in the middle, and I took a deep breath, but he continued upwards toward my belly button. Then he licked from my belly button to my breast. He unhooked my bra, and went to work on each breast. He stopped abruptly, which caused me to open my eyes. He stroked my cheeks, and my chin, and said, "Baby, I love you, I just want to show you how much, will you let me?" I was about to answer and he put a hand to my lip. I wrapped my arms around him, and kissed him. I was wondering at that moment, was it possible to love someone the way I loved him? Love seemed like it wasn't even enough to describe what I felt for him. I knew at that moment that I would do anything to keep him, and I meant it.

Bernard told me to close my eyes because he had a surprise for me. He jumped off the bed, and came right back. He told me when to open my eyes. He was holding a long jewelry box in his hands. He opened it and revealed a name plate chain that said Bernard loves Joanne with a diamond in between our names. He said he was proud of me, and he wanted me to wear the chain everyday, so I could have a reminder of how much he loved me. I didn't even realize I was crying until I felt the wetness on my cheeks. He wiped my tears and hugged me tightly. I whispered I love you into his ears. I climbed on top of him and started kissing his chest. I pulled his boxers off and took him into my mouth, and I couldn't believe how much I liked doing this now. His moans let me know how much he was enjoying this, and I was happy to please him. When he came, it was so intense. He flipped me over and practically tore off my panties, and returned the favor. After a while, I couldn't take it anymore and I demanded that he put it in immediately. He started pumping slowly then quickly, and I thrust back slowly then quickly. Right before I came, I let out the biggest scream, I hoped that no one heard me. He kissed me and wrapped his body around me. I could have stayed like that all night. Bernard was nowhere in sight when I woke up, but a few minutes later he came back into the room and served me breakfast in bed.

When I got home, I went straight to my room, took off my clothes and jumped in bed. It felt like last night had been a dream, but then I touched the necklace around my neck and knew it was real. I fell into a deep sleep, and didn't wake up until six that afternoon. I walked into the living room to find Bernard there talking to my brother. I looked like a mess, and there he was smiling at me. I knew I should have been embarrassed, but I wasn't. He would have to see me in less desirable situations. He came over and kissed me on the cheek. I went back upstairs to shower, and threw some sweats and a t-shirt on, and went back downstairs to join Bernard.

Bernard asked me if my parents were home, and I didn't know because I hadn't checked. He leaned in and gave me a quick kiss. I had one last final exam to take, so I had to study. He asked what I had planned, and I told him I had to study for my exam the next day. He walked with me to Dominique's house since we were going to study together, and what should have been like a five-minute walk turned into half an hour because we took the long way, and stopped at the park. We sat at the park for a while and kissed and felt each other up like junior high school kids. I pulled him up to go because if I had stayed another minute, I wouldn't have made it to Dominique's house or for my final the next day.

Dominique was already at the table going over her chemistry notes for the test and she was looking over the Barron's Regents book. I went to the table and dropped my books down. Bernard sat down at the table, and we both looked up at him. He got the hint, and left to go find something to do. Dominique's family was watching a movie in the living room, and he joined them. Before she went back to her notes, she complimented me on my chain and asked what time I got home. We talked for a while and then got down to business. When we were done, Bernard walked me home, and we talked outside for a while because I knew if he came in, I wouldn't want him to leave. When he decided to leave, he drew me into a warm embrace, and left. I stood there for a while, and watched him as he drove off in his rental. I went inside and went straight to bed.

Monday's Chemistry Regents exam was a killer, but I was confident that I passed. After the test, Dominique and I went out to eat and celebrate our last exam, and the fact that Wednesday was our graduation. We would be nearing the end of high school officially. After hanging with Dominique, I went to Bernard's hotel.

He answered the door with a towel wrapped around his waist. His hair was still a little wet, and he smelled nice and fresh. He pulled me inside in one quick motion and let the door close. I was barely inside when he began kissing and stroking me. We lay there for a while, before he pulled me up to the shower with him, and we went for round two. That day was a lazy afternoon spent in the hotel exploring each other's bodies and making up for lost time.

On Tuesday, I got my hair done for graduation. I wrapped my hair, so that my cap would fit easily over my head. Then I did some last-minute shopping in search of a pair of shoes to match my outfit. When I got back home, Bernard was waiting for me and no one else was around. He said my brother let him in on his way out. My parents were still at work, so we had the house all to ourselves. He reluctantly followed me upstairs, when I started rubbing him the right way. We didn't have much time, so he barely pulled down his pants and slid my underwear to the side and slid inside of me. Afterwards, we headed back downstairs, and I started dinner. It was hard for me to concentrate on dinner with him so close by and me fighting him off because he couldn't keep his hands off me.

Halfway through cooking, my mom came home, greeted Bernard and retired to her room. By the time my dad came home, dinner was ready and I called my mom downstairs and we all ate. After dinner, we watched tv, and I had my legs on his lap. I was telling him that I would probably make it to Florida by the end of July because I wanted to spend some time with my friends and family before I left. It was an early night because I had to prepare for graduation the next day.

Graduation was set for nine in the morning, so the graduates had to be there by eight. Bernard drove Dominique and I to graduation, and I was so excited because the big day was finally here. Four years of memories to think back on. When my name was called, I looked towards my family and there was Bernard snapping pictures which made the moment even more special. After graduation, we went back to Dominique's house because she was having a graduation party. Bernard would be leaving early the next day, so we wouldn't have time for a long goodbye. We sat there in the park, and he seemed really deep in thought, little did I know that he was thinking about the truth of his situation that I knew nothing about. When I noticed the faraway look, and asked him about it, he said it was nothing, and that he was just thinking about how much he was going to miss me, and that he needed to know that I would be there for him no matter what. In response I said, "I will always be here for you." We sat there a while in silence, each person lost in their own thoughts. Finally, we walked back to Dominique's house, and he gave Dominique a teddy bear that said congratulations, and hugged her goodbye. I walked him out to the car, and hugged him for a long time. He held me really close, kissed my cheeks, and got in the car. Thursday, Bernard came to my house before his morning flight. I wanted to go with him to the airport, but he insisted that I didn't go because he said it would be more difficult for him to get on the plane if I were there. I kissed him with all the passion and longing I already felt.

The Sunday before I left Dominique, Stacey and I went out to celebrate me leaving in a few days. We were leaving Sony theaters when she met him, the guy who would become the love of her life. Dominique stayed with him, and Stacey and I left. We strolled around and enjoyed the rest of the afternoon together. At first, I felt a little dissed that my girl just left to go off with a stranger, but I understood because I was going to college away from my friends to be closer to Bernard. Stacey came back to my house and helped me pack for Florida.

My parents were also going with me to help me get settled in. Since we had a home in Florida, I would stay there and drive to school. My parents bought me a car as a graduation gift because they knew driving in Florida was necessary. Since there was still a month before school started, I got a job at the mall to keep myself occupied since Bernard had a busy schedule. He seemed happy that I arrived but also very distant. Either way I brushed it off…

7

OH, WHAT A SUNDAY!

Dominique

IS THIS LOVE *in the air for Dominique or is this just the smell of popcorn? Dominique made it very clear that she isn't a long-distance relationship type of girl. But it looks like someone in her town is here to sweep her off of her feet.*

It was a beautiful Sunday afternoon in June, when my life changed in so many ways. Joanne and Stacey, my two best friends and I had decided to go to the movies. We went to the Sony Theater on 68th street in the city. We loved strolling through the neighborhood afterwards. We were going down the escalators, and he was coming up. Our eyes locked, and I felt this electricity between us. I know it sounds crazy, but that's what I felt. We kept our gazes on each other, and I couldn't hear anything that my friends were saying. All I could do was think about the stranger with the red Polo t-shirt, red Polo hat, dark blue Guess jean shorts, and clean Timbs on. He was bald with a beautiful complexion and smooth skin like Tyson Beckford. I noticed that when he got to the top of the escalators, he was still looking my way, and I in my boldness waved for him to come down. By now my friends noticed that I was not paying attention to them and followed my gaze to see what caught my full attention. I didn't take my eyes off of him. He came down the escalators and asked me my name, and the rest was history.

His name was Kenneth and he said it in a voice that I thought was the best I ever heard. "How old are you," I asked. He told me he was twenty-one. He was a junior at City College majoring in Computer Science, and he worked as a computer technician. His job required some travel, which he did when school was not in session. The more he spoke, the more I knew I wanted him. We had light banter, when he asked, "So what movie are we going to watch?" With that question alone, I should have known what I would be in for, but even if there were any warning signs, I would have ignored them. By this time, my friends decided to introduce themselves to him because they noticed I had forgotten they were there. Before I had a chance to say anything smart, he asked me about myself. I told him I was eighteen, and that I just graduated from high school, and was about to attend a University in lower Manhattan in the fall for Business Administration. I said, "What are "we" about to go and see? His reply was simple and smooth, *it didn't matter because I didn't think we were going to pay any attention to the screen.* He was bold, but I found it exciting. To be polite, he asked if my girls wanted to join us.

My girls saw the sparks flying between us and declined. They told him he better not do anything crazy, and I walked them out. They sensed my excitement and told me to be careful. I met him upstairs by the concession stand. I was a little nervous because I didn't want to seem too pressed to Kenneth, but at that moment I just wanted to go with the flow. I was so happy with my outfit that day. I was wearing a black Guess jean skirt, a red cropped Guess t-shirt, red reeboks, and a black denim Guess bag that matched my skirt. My hair was back in a ponytail so my facial features were accentuated. I had a nice caramel complexion with smooth skin, my eyes were shaped almost like perfect almonds, and my lips were full and kissable. I wondered if he had a girlfriend, but realized if he did, it wouldn't be for long because I was already laying claim to him.

The movie he selected didn't start for another hour. Since we had time to kill we took a walk and talked. As soon as we started walking, I asked him the question I had been dying to know the minute I laid eyes on him. I said, "So Kenneth, do you have a girl-friend?" He said, "Do you have a man?" I replied, "that depends …" He walked right into my trap, and asked, on what? I spoke slowly so that he could stare at my lips, "depends on if you have a girl." He caught my drift and laughed real confidently. He said yeah I have a girl, and he must have seen how crushed I looked because he quickly said *you*. Just like that, I was his girlfriend. A real wide smile spread across my face and I leaned in and kissed him.

I don't know where all this boldness was coming from, but there was just something about Kenneth that made me lose my mind. Wow! I had a boyfriend. That's how simple it was or so I thought. I don't even remember the name of the movie we saw cause all we did was make out in the movie theater. I had been kissed many times before, but I had never been kissed like this. Every nerve in my body was on fire. I was tingly all over. Everything felt so intense while kissing Kenneth. At that moment, I knew this man would have my heart forever.

WHAT MY PARENTS DON'T KNOW...

Joanne

I HUGGED MY PARENTS goodbye, and waited until their plane took off. Then I turned to Bernard and told him to lead the way. We couldn't get there fast enough. The first time we only got as far as his hallway, the second time, we made it to the living room, and then finally we made it to his bedroom. I didn't have to be at work until eleven, and Bernard didn't have a client until later in the afternoon. I woke up at about eight. Bernard was still sound asleep, so I went to the bathroom, and showered and thought he would be awake when I came back in the room, but he wasn't. He slept naked, so I took him in my mouth until I felt him come alive. He smiled, "breakfast?" He pulled me up, and kissed me with his morning breath, and I didn't mind at all. He got on top and slid inside me, and it felt so good. I got up and made breakfast, serving him in bed, and then I left. I had to go home and change my clothes before I went to work.

By August, I was practically living with Bernard. I went home just to check my messages, mail and get more clothes. He would get upset when I went home to get clothes, and said he didn't know why I didn't just bring my stuff over. Everything was going great, we went out a lot, and spent most of our time just enjoying each other. Registration and freshman orientation was a week before school started. I cut back on my hours at the mall, so that I could focus on school because my parents were not paying for school to have me come home with anything less than a B. My first semester, I had a lot of introductory courses, and the course load wasn't bad. I made a few friends that I talked to in passing, but I knew it wouldn't go beyond school.

When November rolled around, I was torn between wanting to go home, and staying and spending my first Thanksgiving with Bernard. I hadn't made any final decisions, but it looked like I was leaning towards staying in Florida. It was about a week before Thanksgiving when things took a turn for the worse. One night when Bernard thought I was asleep, I heard him talking on the phone in the living room. I wondered whom he was talking to at this time of night. It was midnight, and the only person that Bernard really seemed to talk to was Wesley or his family. Before I could stop myself, I quietly picked up the receiver and heard a woman on the other end. He was telling her that he would not be spending Thanksgiving with her because he had other plans. "What's her name?" Bernard didn't respond. I laid in the bed fuming, who was this woman and why did she want to be with Bernard for Thanksgiving, where had she been all this time. They spoke some more, but I wasn't paying attention anymore. Bernard walked in the room and found the phone in my hand. He hesitated a moment before coming towards me.

I didn't want to look at him. All I could manage to say was, who is she? Then I looked at him and he turned away. He reminded me that I promised I would be there for him no matter what. As if we really meant it when we made those promises I thought to myself. I knew I wasn't going to like whatever came out of his mouth next. He was quiet for a long time, then he confessed, "she's my wife". Wait! Did I hear him correctly? How could he be married? We were practically living together. He explained, "I told you I would always be honest with you, I just didn't know how to tell you this." *Was I in a relationship with a married man? Did that make me a mistress?*

He sat on the edge of the bed and started telling me his sob story from the beginning. They were married right after he graduated college because she was three months pregnant, and he felt it was his responsibility although he did not love her. *He had a kid too?* She had a miscarriage, and when he approached her to get a divorce, she took sleeping pills and tried to kill herself. *Why didn't she die?* Instead of going through with the divorce, he left.

They had been living apart ever since, but she refused to give him a divorce with hope that he would come back. Okay, I could deal with this, I thought. "Why didn't you tell me this before?" He asked if I would be here now if he did? I don't know, maybe yes, maybe no. You should have given me the choice to decide. "I love you, I don't want to lose you." He pleaded. I shook my head in disbelief, "I need to think about this." *Please don't leave me.* I couldn't answer right away. I told him I needed to think. Even though we were in the bed together, we felt a thousand miles apart at that moment. So many thoughts raced through my mind. Would I ever be able to trust him again? Our entire relationship was built on a lie. I decided going home for Thanksgiving would be best. It would give me time away from him, time to think and I would be surrounded by my loved ones.

BLISS

Dominique

FOR THE FIRST six months, everything was good with Kenneth. We spent a lot of time together. In the beginning, my parents objected to the relationship, but I didn't care. Kenneth had become my world. I couldn't make a move without thinking about him. My mother didn't like him, and I resented her for it because I didn't think she had a reason not to like him. She offered me these words of wisdom that I wished I had listened to. She said men can't be trusted, and to make sure I was with someone who loved me more than I loved them. I didn't even know what she was talking about because I loved the butterflies I had in my stomach whenever I saw Kenneth. It's not that I thought I knew it all, I just felt that I knew it all about me and Kenneth, and that she was wrong about him. Looking back maybe my mother sensed something that

I didn't or saw something I didn't because her words came back to haunt me. Anyway, he was the only thing on my mind all the time. It is a wonder I was able to continue doing well in school. I had always been able to focus on school, despite what relationship I was in, but with Kenneth everything was just so intense. If he was upset, I would get upset too, if we were arguing then I would be mean to everyone around me. When things were good, I was feeling good, and when they weren't, I was moody.

During that time, I wanted to spend all my free time with Kenneth. Looking back, I guess there were things I should have paid more attention to, but I was too in love to take a step back and really look at the situation. Everything was just so intense, the sex, the conversations, just everything about the relationship. I remembered the first time Kenneth and I made love to each other. We had been together for four months then, and I was at his house. We were in his room watching videos, when he suddenly turned the tv off, the room was dark except the light coming in through the curtains. We were lying on the bed, and he started kissing me with this intensity that was different than usual. My body reacted so strongly to his touch that the flood gates opened up down there, and I couldn't wait for whatever was coming next. He took my shirt and jeans off, and kissed every inch of my body. He took off my bra with one snap, and he gave each of my twins the attention that they demanded. He sucked on my breasts with a passion and then bit them, and it felt so good. He stopped and turned me around. He massaged my back and every part of my body with his tongue. He touched places that I didn't even know could bring pleasure. He turned me around again and took my panties off and slid his head downtown.

First, he kissed it, then he stuck his tongue and sucked on my clit like it was the last thing he would do. He licked and sucked until I couldn't take it anymore and came. After that performance, I lay there spent, my body just trembling. That was my first orgasm, and it felt good. I was ready to sleep, but he was just warming up. He started the process all over again, and just when I couldn't take it anymore, he slid inside of me. He was large, and it hurt at first. He asked me if I wanted him to stop. I almost screamed, NO!, but I just shook my head instead. He pumped slow then fast, and I flexed my muscles in response to him. I found his rhythm and we moved together. When he came, I felt connected to him in a way I never had with anyone else. He was the first person I ever let come inside of me. He laid there and held me. I knew then that this was where I always wanted to be. I never felt such a strong connection with another man. I thought I would do whatever it took to keep him in my life forever. He told me he loved me that night, and I said it back. We fell asleep in each other's arms. Things were great, but as they say all good things come to an end.

10

HEARTBROKEN

Joanne

MY PARENTS KNEW that something was wrong when I got home, but they didn't push. They asked why Bernard didn't come, and I said because he was working. I called Dominique, but she didn't pick up, so I went to Stacey's. She told me Dominique was probably with Kenneth. I was so caught up with Bernard and school that I didn't really know how things were going with the two of them. I needed to get this huge secret off my chest, so I told Stacey. She was speechless and shocked. This was an emergency, so she called Kenneth's house. We didn't care what we were interrupting because I needed to speak to Dominique. Dominique sounded like she was about to curse the caller for interrupting her flow, when I spoke quickly and said, "I'm home, at Stacey's house come over now this is an emergency." Dominique arrived about forty-five minutes later. I didn't even realize I was crying, as Dominique wiped my tears away and hugged me. I couldn't stop crying, so she looked towards Stacey. I nodded, and Stacey told her.

When she got over her shock, she asked when did I find out, and I calmed down enough to tell her the whole story. She said, "he loves you Joanne that much is clear, so maybe you should give him a chance to work this out." I wanted to agree with her, but how could we work this out? In the meantime, no matter which way I looked at it, he would still be married. She rubbed my back, until I let all the tears out. We were all quiet, when I said I love him with all my heart, and I will never love anyone else like him, but I have to end it. They both told me to think about it and not make a rash decision. Dominique called Kenneth to tell him that she was going to stay at her place. I could see the look of love on her face, and I missed Bernard. How was I going to walk away? Not only was Bernard in my heart, he was a part of me.

I slept at Dominique's place that night. I needed someone close by that I could talk to. I called my parents and they told me Bernard had called several times. It was like midnight when her phone rang, and Dominique signaled me, and I took the phone, and it was him. He said, "hi baby, I wanted to make sure you got in okay." I didn't respond. He said, "I miss you, and I love you, can you please forgive me, and give me another chance?" Tears were rolling down my cheeks, as I hung up the phone. I needed time, and he wasn't making it better. The phone rang again, but Dominique let the answering machine pick up until she heard Kenneth's voice, then she picked up. They talked for a while, and then Dominique said love you too, and hung up. She asked if I wanted to talk about it. I told her what he said, and she reached over and hugged me. I needed that.

I dreaded going back to Florida, but I had to face Bernard sooner or later. I didn't tell him when I was coming because I didn't want him to pick me up. I took a cab from the airport to my parents' house. I found him in the living room and regretted at that moment he had a key. "What are you doing here?"

"Joanne, I know you are still upset, but we need to talk."

"I don't have anything to say to you except, it's over!" *Did I just say that?* He begged, "how can you say that, baby, look how good things were between us."

"You're a married man and a liar."

I wanted to run into his arms and hug and kiss him, and act like everything was okay, but I couldn't. I walked past him and left him standing there. When he heard me slam the door upstairs, he left.

Bernard didn't call for two weeks. I couldn't eat, sleep, or think about anything but him. I was missing him terribly, my body was craving his touch, my heart was craving him, my ears were longing to hear his voice. I sometimes dialed his number to hear his answering machine, if he picked up, I would hang up. I called Dominique and Stacey every night during those two weeks, and I know they were both tired of me, but I didn't have anywhere else to turn. Dominique threatened me that if I didn't call him, she would. I knew she was serious, so I started thinking about what I would say. It was going into the third week and still no word from Bernard, when I decided I couldn't take it anymore. I went to the mall to get the things I would need for what I had planned. It was a Saturday, and I knew Bernard wouldn't be home until about five. I went to his place and got things ready.

On the door, I left him a note, "I miss you, let me show you how much." When he walked in, there was soft music playing, and a bouquet of red roses on the table with a candle lit, and his favorite meal. I sat in his chair with a black lace bra and matching panties. He smiled, and started to speak, when I put my hand to his mouth. I wrapped my arms around him, and he hugged me back. I took his shoes and socks off, undid his shirt, so he could get comfortable. I told him to sit down and eat before it gets cold. He made it a point to mention that he would but there are more important things to do. He carried me to the bedroom, and took the rest of his clothes off and sat me on his lap. He started kissing me, and I couldn't even remember why I was mad or why I thought breaking up with him would solve the problem. Afterwards, we laid there spent, and he spoke first. "Baby, are you sure about this?"

"I just know that you are where my heart is, and I couldn't stand being away from you for this long."

He kissed me, and said, "how about that dinner now."

I reheated it for him, and we ate. When we were done eating, we went and sat on the couch. I told him that knowing he was married was difficult for me to deal with, so he had to get a divorce as soon as possible. He said he would, and we left it at that.

When Christmas rolled around, we were back to our normal routine, and our problems were behind us. I didn't go home for Christmas. Instead, we celebrated our first Christmas together. We exchanged gifts on Christmas eve/Christmas at midnight. Bernard bought me four gifts, and I bought three presents for him. He bought me lingerie, and I thought that was more of a gift for him, but it was thoughtful. He got me a gift certificate to the mall. He got me a mini album with pictures of us from the beginning, and the last gift was a diamond promise ring, that we would get married as soon as his divorce was final because he never wanted to lose me. He placed it on my right hand, and said when the time was right, he would put it on my left hand. I got him some cologne that turned me on whenever I smelled it, a bathrobe, and the matching bracelet to his chain.

The semester ended and I was glad when grades came in, and I passed all my classes with four A's and one B. I called my parents immediately, and they were proud of me. Bernard took me out to celebrate the happy occasion. He ordered drinks for me and I was slightly buzzed as this was my first time drinking. Our love making that night was amazing.

11

GHOSTED

Dominique

WHENEVER KENNETH WAS out of town, he always called me, so him being away didn't bother me much. If I paged him, he would call me right back, and if he didn't that meant that he was busy at work or so I thought. Kenneth had a tough exterior, but was a teddy bear beneath the surface. He spoiled me, and I never had to ask him for anything. If he saw me looking at something, he would get it for me. He would give me money to get my hair done every week because he liked when I looked good, and I think he liked that other men wanted me, but he knew I had no interest in them. Maybe because he was so good to me, I didn't notice it at first when things started to change. It never occurred to me that sometimes he bought me things out of guilt because I was used to him buying me things. Things took a dramatic turn when he went away and didn't tell me. He was away for two weeks and I couldn't reach him. I felt sick to my stomach wondering if he was okay or what could have happened to him. After his two-week disappearance, he called me up one morning as if we had spoken the night before. I was confused. When I asked him what happened, he simply said he was working and didn't offer any more information. Soon after that, Kenneth seemed very distant at times, and when I beeped him, he no longer called me back right away, and his nightly phone calls started dwindling.

After Kenneth graduated, he got a promotion at his job, and took me out to celebrate. Although I was excited, this new position would require him to travel a lot, and he didn't seem to mind. I didn't mind either because I trusted Kenneth and thought he would keep his mind on work. Kenneth was away for our anniversary that year, but he sent me two dozen red roses with a Happy Anniversary balloon, and a giant card with our picture on it. I was so touched and I couldn't wait to see him. He called me that night and said he would be home in two weeks and said he would have a surprise for me and we could celebrate then.

When he got back, his surprise was a 14k nameplate chain with our names on it. I gave him a watch he was eyeing and a Polo Sport cologne because it was one of his favorites. It was hard to shop for him because he had everything. We went out to eat, and went back to his place afterwards. Kenneth had just moved into a two-bedroom apartment, and it was really nice. He hadn't bought any furniture yet, so we went straight to the bedroom. It had been about a month since Kenneth and I had been intimate. The first time he came quickly, but the second time was a lot better. The second time around, he took the time to please me. We kissed for a long while and he attacked my breasts, slid his head downtown, and then as usual when I couldn't take it anymore, he slipped it in.

I spent the night. He called out from work the next day, and we went furniture shopping for his apartment. He said since I would be spending a lot of time there, I should pick out what I liked because he wasn't much of a shopper anyway. We got an Italian leather sofa, with a coffee table and a nice rug. We went to an art store and bought some black paintings. He bought one with a man and woman intertwined, and it was really nice. The other was with a mother breast feeding her child. He also bought an African mask. We were tired and decided to have lunch before shopping for a dinette set.

We found a small café to have lunch. We talked and he told me about his last work assignment in Atlanta. I couldn't believe it had been a year since we first got together. It didn't seem like we would ever break up. Sure, being with Kenneth was difficult at times, but we always made things right. I knew that Kenneth really loved me. Kenneth told me before he met me, he didn't see anyone exclusively. We had a great connection, so he wanted to move differently with me. Most women didn't hold his attention, and that he got a kick of knowing he could get a girl to do whatever he wanted her to do. There was something about me that made him want to get to know me and take things slowly. He said I was his first love. At the time, I knew he was my first true love, and I would later realize that he was also the love of my life, but that we were not meant to be.

That day, Kenneth asked me to move in with him. I was shocked. I was only nineteen, and my parents would not be pleased with my decision, so I decided to move in with him unofficially and not tell them. Since I didn't go away for college, my parents rented an apartment for me near campus, so I could have the experience of being away and having my own independence. I decided I would keep my apartment, and move in with Kenneth. Stacey spent a lot of time there, so I told her she could stay. That way, if things went wrong with Kenneth, I would still have a place to stay. As I was processing all of this in my head, he sat there staring at me. He said I could use the second bedroom as my study. I was so excited, I couldn't wait to get back home and show him how happy he made me.

When we got home, I put the shower on and let the water run. I undressed him and led him into the shower. Once in, I started kissing him, and then I started licking and kissing his neck. I kissed his chest muscles, then I slid my head downtown, until his manhood was at attention. He moaned loudly, and the more he moaned, the harder I worked. I took all of him into my mouth and believe me that was quite a task. I was down there for what seemed like an eternity before he finally came. I washed his body and he washed mine, then we went into the bedroom. I started the process all over again, and then I straddled him and just let everything out on his body. I let out every feeling and emotion that I had in my body. I felt him coming and came with him. We were both drained afterwards, and we just laid there and held each other. Kenneth was surprised. I had never taken charge like that before. He was smiling, and said he could get used to that. It was still early, and we were both hungry. We ordered pizza. He went to the door when the pizza came, and brought the pizza back to the room. We ate in bed. He said he didn't feel like going to work the next day either, and I wasn't any help because I didn't have to be anywhere the next day. We fell asleep, and I was awakened in the middle of the night to find him inside me which was a nice surprise. I wondered if this was what living together would be like, and if it was, I was definitely looking forward to it. I was fully awake and definitely turned on, so I let him know that I wanted another round. Of course, he was more than willing to oblige me. When we woke up in the morning, I made breakfast, and we decided to finish furniture shopping.

We wanted something simple to put in the kitchen. Kenneth wanted to go to the electronics store of course because he wanted a new entertainment system for the living room. He wanted to get a 52" TV and a new stereo system with huge speakers. We spent a long time there, but I don't think he noticed that. We headed home to eat. I made mashed potatoes and fried chicken. Afterwards, I went home to get some clothes, and Stacey was there, so I told her all about the good news, and she was happy for me and because she would have my apartment to herself. If my parents called, she would call me on three-way. They didn't call me much because I usually called them before they could call me. I hung out with Stacey for a while and went back home to Kenneth. When I got there, he was already laid out in the bed watching tv. I went and took a shower, and in the middle of my shower, he came in. He repeated the process of everything I had done to him the night before. He kissed me, and he kissed my ears, my neck, my back, my stomach, my thighs, and then slid downtown. Then, he turned me around and slid in from the back. I put my hand up against the bathroom tiles and took him in and loved every minute of it. It felt nice having the hot water run down our bodies with him inside me at the same time. We washed each other and went to bed.

He woke up at five to be at work for seven. He woke me up too, because he wanted some loving before he left. I was wondering how long this bliss would last and my answer came soon enough. I cleaned the house, did laundry and cooked. I made macaroni and cheese, baked chicken and prepared a salad. I thought it was time I look for a part time job because I wanted to contribute something to the household even though he didn't ask me. My parents would find that strange because they gave me whatever I wanted as long as I gave them good grades in return which I did. I would have to make sure that my grades didn't suffer with this job when the fall semester started.

I found a job in August at an office. They were very flexible with my schedule. I mostly did light office work like filing, faxing, and answering phones. With the money I earned, I bought groceries for the house, and little things to decorate with. The rest of the money I saved. Kenneth gave me money to go to school, and bought me stuff, so I was good in that department. Living with Kenneth was good. We spent time together, we didn't argue that much, we gave each other the necessary space, and sex was better than ever. When Kenneth wasn't at home, he was at work. I figured if living together wasn't hard then being married wouldn't be that hard either. The way things were going, I figured Kenneth and I could get married after I graduated college in about three years.

12

PICKING UP THE PIECES

I WAS BACK IN school, and everything was going well. I did well that semester as well, and my parents were proud. Bernard took me out to celebrate, and I got tipsy again. The next morning, I woke up with a headache. Bernard gave me some Tylenol and told me to go back to sleep. He called my job, and said I wouldn't be in that day.

When I woke up, it was around six o'clock and I was still tired, so I went back to sleep. When Bernard woke me up, and fed me he said no more drinking for me. When I got home that night, Bernard was already there waiting for me. He said he missed me, and I led him to the bedroom to make up for the past two nights.

In July, I woke up one morning feeling nauseous, and ran to the bathroom just in time to throw up. I knew what was wrong with me because I remembered not taking my birth control pills for three days after the last time Bernard took me to celebrate I didn't have my new prescriptions. My cycle did not come for the month of July. I went out and bought a home pregnancy test, and the results were positive. I left the test on the table and sat in the dark. When Bernard came home, he turned the lights on and found me sitting in the dark. I pointed to the table. He had no clue what I was talking about at first. He picked up the applicator, and then he saw the plus sign. It finally registered to him. "Oh my God, are you pregnant?" I couldn't tell if this was a good thing or a bad thing for him, but it definitely was a bad thing for me. I mean I was only a freshman in college. My parents would be upset. He came over and pulled me off of the couch, and hugged me, "you know we have to get married, right?" That's when I felt like I had the weight of the world on my shoulders. He wasn't even divorced yet. All this time had passed, and she still had not given him the divorce, so how were we going to get married.

I made up my mind right then he had a month or else it was over. I finally reached my last straw. This wasn't about loving him, or him loving me, this was about the fact that no matter how much love there was between us, he still wasn't free to take our relationship to the next level. Wouldn't I be fooling myself, if I went ahead and had this baby thinking that we would be married someday soon? What if she kept fighting the divorce, how long would I have to wait then? I couldn't do that to myself or this unborn child. I wanted to be married and have a baby. Maybe, I should have thought more about it before, but I didn't and an innocent child shouldn't have to suffer for my mistakes. I told him, if the paperwork was not at least drawn up, and she didn't agree in a month, that I was done. That night, I cried myself to sleep, he held me, but I didn't want to be held. What I wanted was to wake up and find out that this was a bad dream. I thought I found the love of my life, but he wasn't free to be with me.

I moved back to my parents' house. I felt Bernard and I needed space. I needed time alone to sort things out and felt he did too. We still spent time together, but it was different. Everything was different now because I didn't just have myself to think about. When Bernard's situation didn't change, I went to a clinic, and got my situation taken care of. Thinking back to that day takes me places I don't want to go. I rested and cried for a few days, then told my parents I would enroll in a college in NY for the upcoming school year. They had late admissions for students, so I was able to get into a school that took my credits.

My parents didn't question me about what happened. I guess they figured I would talk to them when I was ready. My dad wanted to know if he would get his money back for my tuition fee. I told him I would use the money to pay the tuition at my new school, and buy books and the other supplies I needed. During my days at home, I stayed in my bed and cried all the time. Bernard called me a lot, and most times I just hung up. It was just too painful to speak to him. I had yet to tell him about what I had done. I didn't even tell him that I was not coming back home.

I knew I had to talk to him before school started, so I could focus on school. When I called him, I let him speak first, I didn't know where to start. He asked me how I was doing, and why I left without even telling him. "You did it, didn't you?" I guess he knew me well, and I confirmed that I did. He wished things had been different between us, but that he was willing to fight for what we had. I tried to fight too, but I felt like we were hitting the same brick wall. There was a moment of silence. "Joanne, we could have worked this out somehow, you should have had faith in us." I told him I did what I had to do, and that maybe when he got divorced, we would find our way back to each other. He apologized for hurting me, and I apologized for getting rid of the baby without talking to him. I told him that I would always love him.

UNKNOWN CALLER

Dominique

ONE WEEKEND IN October, I was out with Joanne and Stacey. We went to a party for Stacey's birthday. I was a little worried because it was late, and I hadn't called Kenneth to tell him I was coming home late. It was five in the morning when we got home. I thought about going to my apartment to stay with Joanne, so Kenneth wouldn't really know what time I got in, but I decided against it at the last minute. When I got home, I called out to him. I didn't get an answer. I went to the bedroom, and he wasn't there either. I didn't know what to think. I didn't know if he was out looking for me or if he came home and went out, so I just went to lie down, so that if he did come home soon, it could at least look like I had been there for a while.

I was laying in bed for a while when I heard his beeper going off which was unusual cause he rarely left his beeper home. I followed the noise because it kept going off. When I found it, I looked at the number and didn't notice the area code. I called the number back and a girl picked up on the first ring. I asked if somebody paged Kenneth, and she said she must have paged the wrong person. I asked her if she paged Kenneth and to identify herself, and said her name was Keisha. I asked her if she wanted me to give him a message? She asked who I was. She said she lived in Connecticut, and she met Kenneth when he went out there for work. I asked her why she was paging him at this time on a weekend? She said she needed help with her computer. I asked her if she didn't have anyone else to call. She wasn't trying to cause any problems and said that she would call someone else. I got off the phone wondering if I had overreacted or was I right in asking her those questions. I fell asleep waiting for Kenneth to come home.

He came home in the afternoon around two o'clock. He walked in the room and didn't say anything. I knew he was not about to have an attitude and try to turn whatever it was he was mad at on me. I didn't say anything either and I went into the kitchen. I fixed myself something to eat, when he came in and said he was hungry. I was about to say something smart, but decided against it. When I was done cooking his breakfast, I called out to him that the food was ready. When he came into the kitchen, he seemed to be in a better mood. He apologized for coming home late. He explained that he had been hanging with his boys and had too much to drink so he crashed at his friend's house. He said he was too out of it to call. I asked him about his attitude when he came in, and said he had a lot on his mind, and that's how he ended up drinking so much last night.

He didn't want me to see him drunk, so he stayed at his friend's to sober up. I went over to him and kissed him. I sat on his lap and asked him what was on his mind that he couldn't talk to me about. He needed to clear his head. Of course, I didn't know he had recently cheated on me with Keisha, and that it wouldn't be a one-time thing. "If you want to talk about it, I'm here for you." He kissed me and changed the subject to talk about our plans for Thanksgiving. I didn't really think about it because I figured he would just do what he always did and I would be at my parents' house, and he would stop by in the evening after going to his family. He wanted to do something special since this would be our first thanksgiving living together. I told him I would go to my parents' house, but not spend the weekend, and he could either come with me or go to his mom's house. It would be really hard to explain to my parents why I would not be spending the weekend because I didn't have school, so I would have to think of something.

For Thanksgiving, I went to my parents' house and he went to his mom's house, I told him I would call him when I was ready for him to come pick me up. I got lucky at my parents' house because some relatives had come from out of town and would be spending the weekend, so I told them I would sleep at my place, since it would be crowded, and they agreed. I called Kenneth around eight after the festivities died down. When we got home, I made him stay in the living room and watch tv while I got everything ready in the bedroom. I bought some candles and massage oils to set the mood. I wore a sexy red teddy, and had a blindfold that I wanted him to wear along with a scarf to tie his hands with. When I was ready, I threw my robe on, hiding what I had on underneath. I tiptoed into the living room, "baby close your eyes," I whispered as I put the blind fold on over his eyes. Surprisingly, he didn't resist, like I thought he would.

I led him to the bedroom, "lie down… right here … on the bed." I undressed him seductively, leaving him with just his boxers on. At the count of three, I told him he could take the blind fold off. Dropping my robe to the floor, I stood at the edge of the bed. When he opened his eyes, I could see the appreciation and excitement in them. He started to reach towards me and I said, "you can't touch me unless I tell you to, or else I'll tie you up." I told him to lay down on his stomach. I rubbed my hands together with the oil and started massaging his back. He let out a loud sigh. I massaged him from head to toe, then he turned over, so I could massage his chest. He was reaching out to touch me again, and I gave him a warning look. I teased him by feeding him one strawberry before continuing the massage.

I put chocolate syrup on certain parts of his body and licked it off slowly and seductively. He was reaching out to touch me again, and I gave him another look and a warning that this was his last chance. I took his boxers off. He was already at attention. I took him into my mouth and went up and down slowly then quickly. I was working on him for a while, and I let him come in my mouth. That really turned him on. I could tell he wanted to take over, but I was in my zone. I went and got a warm bath towel and rubbed his body down. I laid on top of him and started kissing him, and I was playing with his tongue, and that drove him crazy. What drove him even crazier was that he couldn't touch me. I kissed his chest and started to rub him back to life, and when he got hard again, I stood him up and took him to the living room. I sat him on the couch, and started dancing in front of him and slowly took off the teddy.

When I was completely naked, I climbed on top of him and rode him until our bodies couldn't take it and we came, him first, and I right after. Kenneth just laid there on the couch and looked at me and said, "what else do you have in you that I don't know about?" Stick around and you will find out. He said he didn't plan on going anywhere. I went into the room, and I heard his pager going off again. I checked the pager and noticed it was the same out of state area code as before. I called the number, and Keisha picked up on the first ring. She hung up when she heard my voice. What was that about, I wanted to leave it alone, but I needed to know why she kept paging him. It was Thanksgiving, so I doubt she was at work, like she had claimed before. Kenneth got up and saw the pager in my hand, and saw the look in my eyes. "Who's Keisha? Don't lie to me either." He didn't say anything at first, "Keisha is a girl from Connecticut and I slept with her once." "WHY IS SHE PAGING YOU?" I told him about the weekend she paged him when he was at his friend's house and told him that I spoke with her then. He said that's why he needed to clear his head and got drunk that weekend because he knew he messed up and didn't want to lose me. I asked him if that was the only time he ever cheated on me. He didn't answer me. How many times did you sleep with her?" He said, "I told you already, it was only one time."

"When else did you cheat on me?"

"It's not important because it was in the past and you never found out." I didn't mean to start crying, but that's what happened. He came over to comfort me and I pushed him away.

I didn't want him to touch me and at the same time I wanted him to hold me and make it all better. I stopped fighting him after a while and gave in to him. He kept saying how sorry he was and started kissing me tenderly. He went down and took each breast in his mouth one by one. He went downtown and licked and sucked until I pushed his head away. When he went to put it in, I asked him to put on a condom. I don't even know if he had condoms in the house because we had never used them. I started on birth control pills while with him. He paused for a minute and said he didn't have any. That's when it dawned on me to ask him if he had used condoms with the other women. "I would never do that to you."

"You cheated, so you did just that to me." The mood was ruined, and I was angry again. "Should I sleep on the couch? "If you sleep in the bed, don't touch me." He slept in the bed.

Usually, we slept naked, but I put my cotton pajamas on and slept with my back facing him, and stayed as far from him as the bed would allow me to go. I decided that I wasn't satisfied with what Kenneth told me, so I got up in the middle of the night and called Keisha at two in the morning. She didn't sound like she was sleeping when she picked up the phone. I guess she thought it was Kenneth calling, but when she heard my voice, she didn't say anything. "This is Dominique, Kenneth's girlfriend, but I guess you already knew that." Kenneth told me about their affair, but I wanted to hear from her what happened. I couldn't believe what this woman was telling me about how she and Kenneth met when he came into her office to work on some computers.

She was attracted to him immediately, which I understood because he was quite attractive, but I never thought about the fact that other women were constantly hitting on him. She decided to speak to him when she saw him for the second time. As she spoke, I wanted to reach through the phone and smack her. She admitted that when she approached him, he told her he had a girl at home. The fact that she didn't care irked me even more and I wanted to scratch her eyes out and do bodily harm to Kenneth. Apparently, he turned her down at first, but she persisted and he eventually gave in when she waited for him outside his hotel room. He told her to leave, then like a man he gave into her and they had sex.

At this point, I was seeing red and asked if he ever called her afterwards. Her silence spoke volumes. Why was she still calling my man then. As angry as I was at him, I was even more irritated with this lady that shamelessly pursued him and continued calling him after he paid her no mind. "I'm pregnant." Those two little words changed everything. I didn't know what to think. So many questions flooded my thoughts. *Was she lying? Was she telling the truth? Was it his? Did they use protection? What if he caught something, did I have it?* To make matters worse she was keeping it. "He doesn't love you, he doesn't even want you." She didn't have the heart to get rid of it, and she just thought he should know. There was nothing left to hear. I hung up the phone.

I stomped angrily to the room and woke Kenneth up out of his sleep. He saw how angry I was, and quickly sat up. I imagined just punching him or pouring hot water on him because I wanted him to feel the gut-wrenching pain I was feeling. "Keisha's pregnant, and it's yours. That's why she's been paging you for the past month." All he managed to whisper was that they used a condom and that she was trying to mess things up between us. "Don't blame her, you messed things up when you cheated." He apologized profusely saying he never meant to hurt me. I don't know if I was seeing things but it looked like a tear rolled down his cheek.

At that moment, I didn't even care. I called a cab and went back to my place. He tried begging me to stay, but I couldn't look at him without crying or screaming at the top of my lungs at him. I had never been unfaithful to Kenneth, so the thought of him cheating never crossed my mind. I mean guys always tried talking to me, but I shut it down. Why did he have to be so weak and inconsiderate? Did he ever stop to think how it would make me feel? Or was he just happy he never got caught?

I knew Joanne or Stacey would be asleep at my place, and I didn't want to wake anyone, so I stayed on the couch and cried until I felt empty inside. I felt like Kenneth had taken away everything in me. I thought I had let it all out, but as the tears kept flowing, I knew I would never feel complete again. I felt like Kenneth completed me, and he took that feeling away from me. I hated him at that moment for doing this to me. He made me feel weak, vulnerable, unloved, needy, and desperate. I remembered my mother's words: never trust a man. Those words came back to haunt me, I found myself asking why hadn't I listened to her, and thought maybe the saying that mother knows best was true. I wished at that moment that I had never met Kenneth. Why would someone who claimed to love you cause you so much pain and hurt? What had I done to deserve this? All I had been trying to do was show this man love the best way I knew how. I tried to think of new things to do to keep things exciting between us. I committed myself to him and our relationship, and it wasn't enough. My train of thoughts was broken when I heard a key at the door.

It was Kenneth! I forgot he had the keys. He came in quietly, and came up behind me and hugged me. I didn't move away from him, nor did I snuggle into him. He heard my tears and said, "baby I'm sorry, I never meant to hurt you. I made mistakes, and I can't change that, but I love you with all my heart." In my mind I said if this is what you do to someone you love with all your heart, you are a monster. Instead, I said, "I came here to be alone." He turned me around to face him and I noticed that he was crying as well. What the heck was he crying for? His tears touched me because I loved Kenneth with everything in me, and I had never seen him cry. At that moment, I hated myself for caring. He wiped my tears and stroked my chin and cupped my face in his hands and kissed me lightly. I kissed him back and we fell to the floor and made love like we were holding on to something that we didn't want to let go of. He wasn't sure if this would be the last time, so he wanted to make it worthwhile.

That night, Kenneth made me feel complete again, but something had died inside of me that I didn't know if I could get it back. I loved Kenneth, and I wanted to make things work, but where were we supposed to go from there. He had a child on the way. *Would he be a part of this child's life? Would I want him to be an active part of this child's life?* That wasn't my decision to make but whatever he decided to do would affect me also. *How was I supposed to trust him again? How would I feel when he was traveling? He didn't want to tell me about the other times he cheated, so how would I know if he were being sincere this time around? How did I know he really used condoms all the time? Didn't Keisha say their condom had broken? How many of those were out there?* So many questions filled my thoughts. We laid there on the floor in silence. He asked me if I wanted to go home because he didn't want to leave me. Why all of a sudden did he want to be up under me? Why didn't he think to call me when he was out there cheating on me?

I asked, "Why did you cheat on me?"

"Do you want to talk about this right now?"

"We might as well." He explained that he cheated on me at the beginning of our relationship because he didn't know how far it would go with us, but that it really shouldn't count because we weren't having sex yet. I didn't even know how to respond, so I just listened. *When did he find the time to cheat and still spend all that time with me?*

I felt like I had fallen in love with a lie and that our relationship was just based on lies. I thought back to him telling me that he would take his time with me, of course he could take his time, he was still having sex with other girls. He said he cheated on me again when he found himself really falling for me because he had never been in love before, and it scared him. I felt like such a fool lying there with him. *Was I that naïve and blind that I missed all of this going on right underneath my nose?* "If you felt all these things, why didn't you talk to me about it?" Then he told me the dumbest thing I ever heard. He said that with Keisha, he did say no at first, but after she kept persisting, he figured this would be his last chance before we got married. That was a loaded statement for me. We never really spoke about marriage, I guess it seemed like that was the next step for us. He said before all this happened, he was planning on proposing to me. Right there he pulled out a nice gold diamond ring and proposed. The ring was beautiful, but what was I supposed to say? I was angry at Kenneth. *How could he do this to me now?* Like a fool, I said yes, but I guess it didn't matter because we would never make it down the aisle anyway.

We made love again right there on the floor, and fell asleep. When I woke up, although I was still angry, I had a new determination now to be with Kenneth. I mean I was willing to do whatever it took to make it work cause he was the love of my life, and I was determined to marry the love of my life and live out my fairy tale. I felt a little weird being in my apartment because I was so used to his place. I went out for breakfast. While he was still asleep, I admired my ring, and I thought about the future that we could have if we worked hard and made this relationship work. I knew the road ahead wouldn't be easy, but I was willing to try if he was. I guess proposing to me really meant that he was willing to try. I watched him as he slept, and thought about how much I loved him, and the fact that I was willing to do whatever it took to make this work. I woke him up, so we could eat breakfast together.

During breakfast, we talked about wedding plans. We talked about getting married after I graduated from college which would also give us a chance to save money. Am I supposed to ask your parents first, or should we tell them together? I guess I hadn't thought that far but as soon as he mentioned it, I felt nervous. What would my mother say? She never liked Kenneth for me, and my father never said much, he just wanted me to be happy. I didn't know if I was ready to tell my parents yet. I guess he saw my facial expression had changed, and he said he was okay with whatever I thought was best concerning my parents. I told him even though I said yes to the proposal, we still had a lot of issues to work on because I no longer trusted him. He wanted a paternity test and would take care of the baby if it was his, but that he didn't want to be a part of her life like that. I mumbled that he should have thought of that before he slept with her. He simply responded that he was aware that he messed up, but throwing it in his face didn't change anything.

While I wanted to be supportive, I also wanted him to understand that things would not be easy with us moving forward. For now, I had to deal with her pregnancy, but the child being born would bring about yet another change in our relationship.

When we got home, he cleaned up the house, and stayed out of my way. When dinner time came, he heated up the leftovers from my mom's, and we ate together quietly, both of us lost in our own thoughts. For the next few days, I gave him the silent treatment, only talking to him when absolutely necessary. To get back in my good graces, he tried to make it up to me by taking me shopping the following weekend. He definitely knew that would win me over. I bought a shearling coat, leather jacket, a few pairs of boots, a few designer handbags, and some new outfits. Retail therapy always felt nice.

I knew he was sorry, but I wanted to see how long this treatment would last. When we got home that evening, I was so tired that I dropped the bags that were in my hand right behind the door. He told me to relax, while he went to run a bath for me, and led me to the bathroom and bathed me. Afterwards, he wiped me down, and led me to the couch and put my feet on his lap, and rubbed the bottom of my feet. I felt so relaxed and turned on, but I didn't know if I was ready to sleep with him. I wanted him to understand that we were not going to pick up from where we left off, and I wanted us to start using condoms. I could see the disappointment in his face when I said as much. As I lay there naked on the couch, I could tell he wanted me to come to the bedroom, but he didn't ask. He went to bed frustrated. This would be a first. He turned the TV on and tossed and turned. I was suffering on the couch, but I couldn't back down, so I turned the TV on in the living room. I wasn't paying any attention to it, but it served as a distraction, to keep me from going in there. I didn't know how long this would last, and I started to ask myself what not sleeping with him was going to solve? *Wouldn't it just push him further away?* No! I blocked those thoughts out because I wanted him to miss what he had, and realize that he came very close to losing it because he couldn't keep it in his pants to begin with.

I don't know what time I fell asleep, but I woke up on Sunday morning to the smell of breakfast being cooked. I went to brush my teeth, and I sat at the table and waited for him to serve me. Breakfast was delicious. He made pancakes, an egg omelet with spinach, home fries and turkey sausage. Kenneth rarely cooked, but when he did, it came out well. He asked what I wanted to do that day. I was just thinking about staying in and relaxing. I told him I wanted quiet time. I needed some space because every time I looked at him, so many emotions filled up within me. I called Joanne to fill her in on the recent events, and after talking to her for a while, I felt a little better. It was hard talking to Kenneth about everything that was on my mind because I felt a lot of anger towards him, and I found that it was easier to talk to my friends because they sympathized and related to the situation as only women could. When Kenneth came home, he came and sat next to me on the couch. He said, "Dominique, I love you and I am sorry, please stop punishing me and come back to bed, I missed you in it last night. We don't have to do anything, I just want to feel your body next to mine." Why was it so hard for me to say no to him? "Baby, I will never cheat on you again, you are the only woman I want and need in my life. I am sorry for the hurt I caused you and I know I can't change it, but I will do my best to not hurt you again." That night in bed, he held on to me tightly. His body felt good against mine. I wanted to feel him inside me, but I fought the urge. I woke up to the sound of the phone ringing. He was calling to wake me up for school and to tell me he loved me. Why did men do the sweetest things when they felt backed up against the wall or when they wanted to be intimate?

When I went into the kitchen, I noticed the note for me on the table saying he loved me, and that I was the best thing that ever happened to him, and he would do whatever it took to get things back to normal. I smiled and felt a renewed sense of hope for our relationship. Things were going good with Kenneth, and for Christmas, we went away for a few days to the Bahamas. Going away was nice, and it was a much-needed vacation. When we came back, we were nice and relaxed and looking forward to ring-ing in the New Year together.

We stayed home on New Year's and just enjoyed each other's company. I cooked and we had a nice dinner by candlelight. After dinner, we ate dessert, and made resolutions for the New Year. One of his resolutions was to be completely honest with me about everything. One of my resolutions was to try and be more patient with him with this whole situation. We had a nice evening and fell asleep in each other's arms. When I woke up, I called my mother to wish her a happy new year. I knew she was still upset with me for going away with Kenneth for Christmas. I spoke to her for a bit, and then asked to speak to my dad. He asked me if I had a good time in the Bahamas, and he asked if I brought him back anything. I told my dad I would bring it by later. I almost slipped and said when Kenneth wakes up, but I figured that my parents knew that I spent a lot of time there, and although my mother hadn't said anything, she had seen the ring that Kenneth had given me. Kenneth and I went to my parents' house together and then he went to his mom's house later to bring them their souvenirs from our vacation.

Things were great for the next few months. For my birthday, he got me an engraved heart necklace.

For our two-year anniversary, we went to Jamaica, but I think it was to ease his guilt because Keisha's delivery date was soon. When we came back from our vacation, things were a little strained because the day would soon be at hand. Keisha gave birth in July, and the paternity test revealed that Kenneth was the father. Keisha named the baby Kenneth Jr. At first, Kenneth felt torn between feeling like he was hurting me, and wanting to be around his son. It was evident that Keisha wanted them to be a family and she moved to NYC to be closer to Kenneth. Kenneth was over the moon about having a son.

After the birth of his son, we were always arguing because everything was about Keisha and Kenneth Jr, and I saw how attached he was becoming to this child that was not ours. The fact that Keisha was so close to us didn't help matters either. Our second room became a study/ baby room. He had a bassinet in there for when Jr. came over. I mean, I preferred it when the baby came over because Keisha was not there. I will admit that it was selfish on my part, but whenever he was having problems with Keisha, I didn't want to hear about it. He said I was shutting him out, and I was still punishing him to some extent, but seeing the child opened up old wounds. It took some time before things started to get better. I decided to give Kenneth a break, after all I had chosen to work things out and stay with him, so it was time for me to get past things, and accept his child. For Christmas, he went crazy with gifts for his son, and me. We rang in the new year on a positive note, and figured that if we made it this far, we could definitely make it for the long haul. Kenneth said, "maybe we should announce our engagement to our families, since we would be getting married the following year."

I was really warming up to Jr., and that made Kenneth happy and I could tell he appreciated it. Part of my issue was that I wanted to be the one to have Kenneth's first child. For my 21st birthday, Kenneth planned a surprise party for me. He actually had exotic dancers. What guy would watch as his girl drools over other men. My friends were shocked and said he was definitely trying to make things work. He said he knew I always wanted to go to a strip show, and he was more comfortable being there. That was one of the coolest birthdays I had. Our anniversary was soon after my birthday, and for our three-year anniversary, he bought me lingerie and a nice evening gown. He rented a limo, to go and see a Broadway show, then had dinner at a really nice restaurant, and the night ended with a night at the Marriott filled with passion and intimacy. Every time I thought making love couldn't get any better with Kenneth, he blew my mind. With all this bliss we were caught up in, I was completely blindsided of the events that would soon take place.

In July, his son turned one, and he and Keisha went out to dinner to celebrate, but I didn't want to go. I sometimes wish I had gone because maybe things would have turned out differently. When he came home that evening, he was quiet, and I noticed he wasn't with Jr. either. He came and sat next to me on the couch where I was seated, and had a real serious look on his face. "Dominique, I'm sorry." I looked at him, and I knew I wasn't about to like what I was going to hear. "I don't have an excuse, but one thing led to another and I slept with Keisha." He said he was just feeling happy about the fact that she gave birth to his son and really felt in awe of her for being such a good mother to his son. At that moment, I felt like I hated him and I blurted out that he was the biggest mistake I made in my life. He kept saying that he messed up and that he was sorry and that he really thought we could make it work because we loved each other. "How many times do you expect me to go through this with you? It's over!" I stormed out because I didn't want him to see me crying. I hailed a taxi to my place and cried uncontrollably on the cab ride home. I couldn't believe that I had just said that. I didn't want it to be over, but what was I supposed to do? I was just beginning to trust him again and he blew it.

Joanne was at my place when I got there, but I didn't feel like talking. I felt numb. She told me that Kenneth had called several times. I called him to tell him not to come by and that I would come by for my things when he was at work and leave the keys on the table. I also told him I would be changing the locks on my place in case he refused to give me back my keys and plugged out the phone. I didn't leave the apartment for the next week. I was a complete mess, and I couldn't sleep, or eat. I stayed in bed all day, watched TV, cried and ate ice cream. Joanne didn't push it because she figured I would talk to her when I was ready. My mom came to see me, and didn't say I told you so like I expected her to, instead she listened as I told her everything. She asked if I was okay, and just kept telling me that everything would be okay. I was shocked because I knew how much my mother disliked Kenneth, but I truly learned that there's nothing like a mother's love.

My mother forced me to shower and eat and convinced me to take a walk and clear my thoughts. I took her advice, and walked to South Street Seaport. I stood by the water, since it calmed me down. I knew I had made the right decision, but I missed Kenneth like crazy. I was so used to sleeping with him at night, and I was craving Kenneth and hating him all at once. He made me feel like he didn't care for me at all, if it was so easy for him to cheat on me. Why didn't he think of me before he cheated? Instead, he got lost in the moment, and tried to make it up to me later. If he knew he would stand to lose me, why did he do it anyway? Did he think I would continue to forgive him after cheating? When I got home, there were a lot of messages from Kenneth, I didn't call him back because there was nothing he could say to change things. I didn't want us to be friends, so as far as I was concerned there was no reason for us to speak.

Kenneth was very persistent, and he came over two weeks later. I refused to open the door and he refused to leave, so I finally let him in. When he came in, he could see how sad I was and he apologized again and again. I was tired of listening to him apologize because I felt like he continued doing things to apologize for. My mind was made up, and him being here and calling me was not going to change anything. All it did was make me feel worse. "You should just be with Keisha since you have a child together and be the happy family she wants." She's been trying to destroy our relationship. This man was blaming her and not taking accountability for his actions. He must have read my thoughts and said, "I know I slept with her, but it was a mistake and I miss you." He couldn't sleep at night because he missed me near him, and he missed coming home to me and was going crazy. Where was all of this energy when he was out there getting caught up in the moment?

Although I missed him as well, I couldn't keep going through this roller coaster with him and getting my feelings hurt. "Would you forgive me if you found out I cheated on you?" He grew quiet. "I need someone in my life who respects me and what our relationship means."

"I am truly sorry, I didn't mean to do this to you, but doesn't it count that I told you the truth?"

"Even if you didn't tell me now, it would have come out eventually."

"What if I waited until after we had gotten married?" I couldn't believe he thought it would have been ok to start our marriage on a lie. I mean, people forget that telling the truth didn't guarantee that things would turn out the way you wanted them to. I told him that I loved him, but that this was really the end of the road for us. There's no moving on for me because I only want to be with you. If that were true, we wouldn't be having this conversation. I could tell he was getting annoyed because things weren't going as he expected, but at that point I didn't really care. I didn't invite him over, nor did I tell him to cheat. Did he expect me to be nice or pleasant? I was going to say whatever came to my mind whether he liked it or not. I could tell he didn't want to leave, but he recognized there was no point in staying. I knew he felt desperate, when he said, "I will do whatever it takes, we can go to counseling if you want." I was tempted to say okay, but what would counseling do?

How would counseling help him to stop cheating or help me trust him again? I didn't want to live my life always wondering what he was doing at that moment, wondering if he was with another woman. Every time he went to see his son, would that be all he did? When he told me something would I believe him? It didn't make any sense because he would resent me questioning him or throwing it in his face all the time, and I would start to resent myself. It wasn't worth it anymore, at least not to me. Kenneth was and would always be the love of my life, but I realized then that I needed more. I needed to trust someone, and I needed stability, and security and most importantly, I needed to feel safe with the person I loved so that my love would not be betrayed. I understood people made mistakes, but cheating broke so many things in a relationship. In this case, it wasn't like he cheated once, it was continuous and that was simply unforgivable. I felt that I was still young and had my whole life ahead of me, and I had simply reached my breaking point in this relationship. I had endured enough and I deserved better than this. Maybe, if I tried really hard it could work, but why did I have to try so hard at making this relationship work? Was he trying? He was the one that cheated several times, and I had forgiven him and was willing to make it work, but if he thought I would continue accepting it, he was mistaken. I wasn't willing to marry someone knowing that I didn't trust them or that even if he regained my trust, there would always be lingering doubts in the back of my mind about his faithfulness.

Being without Kenneth was one of the hardest things I had to do in my life. I had been with Kenneth for three years. It seemed as if everyone before faded away from my mind, and at that moment it seemed like those that came after him would be insignificant. Although I was still young, Kenneth was a major part of my life. We lived together unofficially for two of the three years we were together. *How do you go back to doing things alone after being with someone for a long period of time?* Kenneth had become a part of me, and I thought I was a part of him. I was going through so many changes. I was depressed one minute, and feeling okay the next minute, other times I thought I was feeling better, and then the next minute suddenly broke down. I knew I had to get my act together because school was starting soon.

When school started, I wasn't my usual self. In class, I would drift off and think of Kenneth. Sometimes, I walked through the hallways crying not really caring who saw. I was even distant from my friends because nothing they said comforted me. By this time, Kenneth had stopped calling and all contact between us was cut. Although that is what I said I wanted, it made me feel worse. I felt like he didn't care, was over me, and had moved on, while I was still crying over him. I told myself not to waste any more tears on him because he was probably with Keisha or the next girl. I felt empty without Kenneth and was struggling to deal with the break up because there was not a day that went by that I didn't think about Kenneth. Looking back, I don't know how I made it through that semester, and I couldn't afford to mess up because I only had one semester to go before graduation. Thinking of graduation didn't excite me anymore. Initially the plan was to start planning our wedding after graduation. He was supposed to be at my graduation, but things were so different now. *Why couldn't I marry the love of my life, like I always dreamed I would, when I was younger.*

I was depressed as the holiday season rolled around because this was my first Thanksgiving and Christmas without him. I figured that he was probably with Keisha and Jr. and they were together like a family. I guess Keisha had finally gotten her wish. I spent the holidays with my family, but I couldn't get into the spirit of the holidays. I was hoping that he would call me, but that call never came. I sat there and wondered if he was thinking about me too, and if he was having a hard time being apart from me.

When New Year's rolled around my resolution was to get out of my slump, and graduate. I didn't even want to attend graduation, but my parents had put a lot of effort into getting me to this day, so they weren't going to miss it. When spring semester rolled around, I had finally started to get into the groove of things again because not graduating was not an option. I focused on school as much as I could. Six months had passed since Kenneth and I had split and I still wasn't over it. I thought it was supposed to get easier as time went on, but that didn't seem to be the case for me. The semester went by quickly, and my graduation ceremony and birthday were both approaching. It was my 22nd birthday, and as graduation was getting closer, I thought more about the milestone I would no longer be meeting, becoming Mrs. Kenneth Cunnigham. I wanted to know if I would ever get married because I couldn't imagine myself loving someone else or trying to give them my all like I had done with Kenneth because I felt like my all had not been enough.

OUT WITH THE OLD...

Joanne

ETTING OVER BERNARD was one of the most difficult things I had to do, but here he was three years later at my college graduation. I was happy to see him because I thought this was our chance to finally be together. After graduation, he came with my family to dinner. Afterwards, we went to the Sea Port and talked. I waited for him to tell me that he was finally divorced, and that he wanted to be with me. Instead, he said, "Joanne I still love you, and I wanted to be here on this day with you, and I came to tell you something in person." I felt my heart skip a beat, when I heard him say that he finally got the divorce a year ago, and I was wondering at that moment why he hadn't called me since last year, when he continued and said that he met *someone else* and was married now with a little boy that just turned one. I couldn't believe him. I asked him why did he even come? I was crying, and he wiped my tears away. I hated him at that moment. I mean we haven't spoken in three years and then he just shows up at my graduation to tell me this nonsense. He reached out to caress my face. He paused for a moment and looked at me as if he were looking into my soul. "I will always love you and you will always be a part of me, but I need to move on with my life. I needed to see you one last time to finally close this chapter. The truth is I never recovered from you getting rid of our baby." His wife had restored that part of him again when she gave birth to their son, but felt he needed to see me one last time. I imagined myself smacking him. *Why didn't he push for the divorce with his wife when we were together? How could he start another family while knowing I was single?* I couldn't believe it, why didn't he tell me that then. I knew what I did was wrong, and I have had to live with that guilt everyday since that day. *Why was this happening to me?* The same man broke my heart again. He left me there staring at the water, and it felt like my heart left with him. For a hot second, I thought about becoming one with the water, but that thought went away as quickly as it came. I cried my eyes out that night, and my tears became one with the water. I knew that it was officially over between us, and that all of my secret prayers would not come true. I had to let it sink in. *Why did he feel the need to tell me this in person?*

He wanted closure, but reopened a new wound for me. I was supposed to be happy about starting this next chapter of my life. Yet, here I was crying my eyes out feeling anything but joy. I secretly hoped we would get back together, but I had to accept this new reality and really mourn the end of our relationship. I wondered for the first time if I had done the right thing by getting rid of our baby, and leaving the way I did, but I could not undo what had already been done, and now I had to fully deal with that choice. I would forever have to live with the guilt that I got rid of a part of us and that Bernard was now living happily with another woman and a child. It was too late now for what if's, but at that moment I really wish I knew what would have happened between us if I kept that baby and stood by him until he finally got the divorce and got married like he promised we would. *Was this my fault because I didn't have enough faith and patience in our love?* So many questions and thoughts ran through my mind at that moment. Even after all this time, when I saw him my heart still skipped a beat. I wanted to know when I would find my happiness. I was happy with Bernard. Being with Bernard was the happiest I had ever been with anybody. Bernard was the first of so many things for me, I didn't even know how I would move on from that. *How do you move on when you feel like you would never be complete again? How do you love again when you loved with everything you had to give?*

When I got home, I went straight to bed and tossed and turned and cried all night. I started crying so loudly that my brother came into the room to see what was wrong with me. I told him I just wanted to be alone. He didn't leave my room, and since he saw Bernard at the graduation, he asked me if he needed to go see Bernard. I chuckled a bit and said it wasn't anything like that. My brother wouldn't leave me alone, so I just told him that we broke up. My brother said I would feel better in time, and that I would find someone better one day. He told me to focus on the bright side. I had just graduated from college with a Bachelor's in Nursing at twenty-one, and I was still young and had a bright future ahead of me. He said even though I was hurting, when I finally found that special someone, I would look back on this and see that it wasn't such a big deal. I would have agreed with him had this been about another guy other than Bernard. Bernard was it for me, but I couldn't explain that to him because he wouldn't understand where I was coming from. I don't know what time I finally drifted to sleep, but I woke up to the sound of the phone ringing. It was Dominique on the other end of the line. She wanted to know where I disappeared to after graduation with Bernard.

I didn't feel like speaking to anybody just yet, but maybe if I told someone else it would make me feel a little better. So, I began to tell her the story, and I could tell she didn't really know what to say. She was expecting a happy ending. Dominique was also still mourning the loss of her relationship with Kenneth, and now I knew how she felt. She said, "I should get dressed and we should celebrate by going out for breakfast, and a day of shopping." Dominique had also just graduated from college with a Bachelor in Business Administration. I realized we did have a lot to be thankful for and retail therapy always made us feel better. Stacy met up with us as well, as she had just graduated with a Bachelor's in Criminal Justice and would be studying for the LSAT. For starters, we all needed to buy clothing for upcoming interviews. We each found suits that fit our style. Then we went on to the shoe section, and picked up a few pairs, and then down to bags and accessories. After we left, we were exhausted, but our shopping was far from done. I decided to drive, so we didn't have to worry about taking the train or anything, but parking was going to cost a lot, but we didn't care. Shopping was indeed the perfect cure. It took our minds off whatever our troubles were. We shopped for summer clothing because although no one said it, we were all single and were looking forward to a summer of fun. After shopping, we headed back to Dominique's place to chill. We were all tired so we decided to have a slumber party.

We were all chilling when a friend of Dominique's called. They spoke on the phone for a while, and she told us that her friend gave her someone's number that she thought she would make a good pair with. She told us his name was David, and said her friend only told her the basics because she said if she wanted to know more, she would have to call him and find out.

"Are you going to call him?" I asked.

"I am not sure if I am ready to go there, but I will think about it."

It has been a year since Kenneth, and it's time to move on. She admitted to being scared for so many reasons. She put the number on the nightstand, and changed the subject, and we all started talking about our dream jobs and how much money we wanted to earn.

I got a job working at the hospital where I did my clinicals my last semester of school and the salary was good for a new RN. I worked a lot of hours, so most of the time I didn't even have the energy to think about my depression. It was December when I met a cute medical resident working at my hospital. I saw him from time to time and we would greet each other in passing. On this particular night, the emergency room was full of people, so I knew it would be a long night ahead. When we finally found a moment, we found ourselves in the cafeteria and he bought me a cup of coffee. As he sat across from me, he introduced himself.

William was very attractive. He was 6'2, dark complexion, bald headed, beautiful white teeth, and a nice medium sized build with an inviting smile to match. Although he didn't look like Morris Chestnut, that was the first person that popped into my mind when I saw him because of his features. William said he had six months remaining before he completed his residency. We talked for a bit, and he asked me if he could take me out. I was about to say no, when I realized it would be nice to be in the company of a man because all I did was work these days. I said yes, and gave him my telephone number. I was still living at home, and didn't have time to look for an apartment. Maybe this would be just the kick I needed to get the ball rolling. I went back to finish off my shift, and for the first time in a while I felt like I had something to look forward to.

He called me two days later. I was off, and was thinking about picking up a shift at work, when the phone rang. I knew who it was right away. There weren't any other men calling me. "Can we get together later," his sexy voice said on the other end of the phone. Since it was cold, I suggested that whatever we do, it be indoors. "Let's go ice-skating at Chelsea Piers which has an indoor ice-skating rink. I heard a lot about it, but had never made it there yet." I told him I would be ready in about an hour, and we decided to meet at the train station in the first car.

I wore blue jeans, a red turtleneck and my high boots. I threw on my black bubble jacket, and grabbed my bag before heading out the door. I hadn't told anybody about William, in case he didn't call. I wanted to see how things would go first before I said anything. When I got to Chambers Street, William was already there waiting. He wasn't sure how to greet me, so he just said hi. We got on the next train and rode a few stops to our destination, and walked the few blocks to Chelsea Piers. When we got on the ice, he held my hands as we slid across the ice. I wasn't a great ice skater, but I could skate without falling if no one bumped into me. When they had to clean the ice, we went to have some hot chocolate. I grabbed a table and he came back with some croissants and hot chocolate.

William started telling me more about himself. He was twenty-seven, and he wanted to work in the pediatrics unit of the hospital. He was staying at an off-campus apartment near his school. He didn't have any children, nor had he ever been married. He said with his schedule he didn't have a serious girlfriend although he dated a little when he had time. I told him about myself and he said I seemed mature for a twenty-two-year-old. He was surprised that I wasn't in a relationship and said the cheesy line that if he were my man, he would not let me go. Since it was still early, we decided to catch a movie and then see where the night would lead. So far, he seemed okay, but only time would tell.

After the movie, we talked and headed to the closest restaurant we saw since it was so cold outside. The last time that I was out with a man was… with Bernard. I looked up at William sitting across from me, and he was quite attractive. He had nice thick lips, piercing eyes and a nice physique. I allowed myself to wonder what it would be like to kiss him, and I got a tingly feeling in my stomach. Instead of thinking about how long it had been since I had been kissed, I focused on the fact that I would be kissing someone soon enough. We walked back to the train station, he hugged me as my train was coming in, and went to catch his train. I got on the train in a good mood. I smiled for the first time in a long time and hoped this would be the beginning of something good.

NEW BEGINNINGS...

Dominique

MET DAVID ABOUT a year after the devastation with Kenneth. One evening, a friend of mine called me, and told me that her neighbor had given her his number so that I could call him. She explained to me that he was over her house and saw my picture, and he inquired about me, and she told him that I was single, but anything else he needed to know he would have to ask me directly. Since she didn't want to give him my phone number, she took his instead. I asked her how he looked, and she didn't answer the question, instead, she mentioned that he was smart, nice, and hardworking. I wondered if he had all these good qualities, why he was still single, and if he was attractive, since she mentioned everything but his looks. I wrote the number with no intention of calling him. I put the number on my nightstand, and continued talking to Joanne and Stacey as we were having a slumber party that night.

It was about a month later when I called him. There wasn't anything interesting on TV, and my friends were nowhere to be found. As I turned over on my bed, I saw the number on my nightstand, and thought for a long while whether or not I should call him. I dialed the number, and he picked up on the third ring, as I was about to hang up.

"Hello, may I speak with David please?"

He said, "Hi, how are you?"

I said, "aren't you going to ask who is calling?"

He said, "I already know who it is." I identified myself anyway. We began talking and hit it off. He was very easy to talk to. We asked each other questions about each other, and he answered them all eagerly, but then again it always seems that way in the beginning. We spoke for about two hours. I called my friend who had given me the number right after I got off the phone with David. I filled her in on the highlights of the conversation. I asked her again how he looked, and her reluctance to tell me made me a little worried. Usually, if the person was cute, you said it without hesitation.

I lay in bed that night with a lot going through my mind. *Was I ready to start dating again? Could I trust another man? Would I hold back? Would I push him away? Should I tell him about my past with Kenneth and the heartache he caused? Could I trust my judgment to be better this time around?* It was strange how I went from having a pleasant conversation with what seemed to be a nice man, to having doubts about letting someone get close to me, and becoming a part of my life. I knew that if I got any sleep, it would still be a restless night. Thoughts of the past filled my mind, and it made the pain seem fresh again. I laid there in bed for hours just thinking, and when I couldn't take it anymore, I picked up a book to read.

After flipping through a few pages, my phone rang. I looked at the caller ID to see it was David calling. I picked up on the fourth ring because I wasn't sure if I wanted to talk to him. He told me that he had been thinking about me, and decided to take a chance and call me back. "I hope it isn't too late," he said. It was about ten o'clock and I replied that since I was a late sleeper that it was okay. He didn't want to seem too forward, but he wanted to know when we could meet in person. I was extremely curious about how he looked, but I wasn't sure if I wanted to meet him just yet. What if I wasn't attracted to him? I didn't want to seem uninterested either because after all he seemed like a nice guy from our conversation earlier. Can we meet after work at a coffee shop or have dinner? I thought about the coffee shop because if I didn't like him in person, I could cut our conversation short since it was more casual, but dinner seemed appealing too because I had not gone out on a date since Kenneth, and if I liked him we would have a chance to talk. I told him we could meet later in the week for dinner. That would give me a few days to wrap my mind around going out on a date again. He asked me if there was a particular restaurant I wanted to go to. I told him that we could go to the Olive Garden. "I will pick you up at work then." If I was being honest, I felt a little nervous and excited about meeting David.

As soon as I got home from work the next day, I left messages for Joanne and Stacey. Within the hour, Joanne called back. As usual, she gave me great advice. She told me to treat David as an individual, and not to judge him for the men in the past, and to listen to what he said. We talked for about an hour when the other line beeped, and it was Stacey returning my call. I told Joanne that if we didn't speak tomorrow, we would definitely talk after the date.

I spoke to Stacey, and she was excited because I finally decided to go out on a date. We spoke for a while, and the phone beeped, and it was David on the other line. This was the kind of thing that annoyed me the most about men. They would call all the time in the beginning, but as soon as they felt secure they had you, their patterns changed. I was happy that he called, but I tried not to make too much of it because it was still early. We spoke and fell into our easy rhythm of conversation. I had to admit talking to him was relaxing and easy. He told me a lot about himself. He told me about his college years, and how he almost dropped out of law school. I didn't say much, I talked about the basics without going into too much detail. He gave me his work, beeper, and cell phone number. He wanted me to be able to reach whenever I wanted. Before, I would have thought this was a good sign, but I knew that only time would tell about David's true character. He assured me that if he wasn't working, then he was at home most of the time. He was just starting at a very prestigious law firm, and told me there were times when he might be really busy with work, if he was working on a particular case. He lived in the city on East 78th street around Lenox Hill hospital and had been living there for about two years. Before we hung up the phone, he told me that he couldn't wait until our date. I smiled. I was a little anxious, but I was not about to tell him that.

The night before our date, I was on edge because I didn't know what to wear for the date. I was going after work, and I didn't want to look like I was going to a business meeting, yet I didn't want to be too sexy for work. I was searching for a cross between classy and business. I decided that I would wear a tan Barami skirt suit with a lace top underneath. After work, I could go from professional to a little sexy once I unbuttoned my blazer. I spoke to Joanne and Stacey and they both hoped that I would relax and just have a good time. David called me that evening, and I was happy to hear from him. It was nice being able to talk to a man again on a regular basis. I had gone so long without a man in my life that I forgot that it could actually be nice having someone to talk to. We had our usual pleasant conversation and he said goodnight early.

The next day at work, I was feeling anxious all day. I thought of calling him many times to cancel because I was so nervous. I wondered what he would look like, and how I would act if I wasn't attracted to him. Good looking men were always my weakness. Of course, one's character was important, but if I said looks didn't matter to me, I would be lying. Physical attraction was very important to me, without it I could not have a relationship with someone. I just hoped I would be attracted to David. He had an advantage since he already knew what I looked like. I didn't have any particulars about a man, just that he was in shape and taller than I. I was 5'8, so I wanted a man who was at least 5'10. Concentrating at work was so hard and time seemed to go by slowly that day.

David called me at work around three to confirm we were still meeting. He said he would call me when he was downstairs. My phone rang at four-thirty on the dot, and David told me he was downstairs, even though he said he would recognize me, he said he was wearing a navy suit with a striped tie.

The elevator ride down was so nerve racking. When I stepped out of the elevators I spotted him immediately, and I was very happy with what I saw. David had dark skin and nice smooth skin and lips that looked like they were waiting to be kissed. He was about 6'4 and I gave him an easy nine, on a scale of one to ten. I was wondering why my friend didn't tell me that he was this fine.

I might have called sooner if I knew. He was dressed impeccably in a navy suit with a French blue shirt and a pin striped tie that brought the two colors out. His shoes were Italian leather, and well-polished. I didn't know how I should greet him, so I settled for a handshake. There was a town car waiting for us outside, and he instructed the driver to take us to the Olive Garden. There was a lot of traffic, but we barely noticed because our conversation was so interesting.

He complimented me on my outfit, and I returned the compliment because he was looking sharp as well. Again, I wondered why my friend hadn't told me that he looked this good. I wondered at that moment why he was still single. He seemed to have a lot going for him, and I could just imagine that he had a lot of admirers. "How is it that you are still single?" He simply said that he was waiting for the right one. He said that although he dated occasionally that work kept him busy and no one had fully caught his attention. He was looking to settle down with one person, and having a family, and saying all the things that serious women wanted to hear.

"When was your last relationship?" He had broken up with someone about two years ago, and had dated a few people after her, but nothing serious. Up until now, I had tried to stay away from those questions because I was not ready to answer them in return. I asked him if there was anything he felt I should know. Although he said he dated very little, I wondered if there was someone out there who thought he was her man. He said at the moment, he was not dating anyone, and there was no one out there that he was tied to. He said he was single and looking to change that with me.

I thought that was a bit strong, but I told him I was also single and had come out of a relationship a year ago, had not dated anyone since, and was not sure what I would want to happen between us. However, I explained to him that if we were to begin dating that I would want it to be exclusive. He agreed to that. We sat in a comfortable silence after putting those things out there. It appeared that David's mother had done a fine job in raising him, unfortunately his parents had passed on, so I would not get the chance to meet them. He told me that his father died of cancer, and his mother died from a lonely heart from missing his father so much in that same year. He was twenty-four when it happened. He said that was why he almost dropped out of Law School, but his family encouraged him to push through since he was almost done. At twenty-eight, he was the youngest of four. He had one brother, thirty-four, and two sisters, thirty-two, and twenty-nine. He said they were close, but didn't spend as much time together like he would want since they all lived in different states. His family was also originally from Haiti, and that was an added bonus being Haitian-American myself. We had similar family values. His family wanted a better life for their kids and migrated to NYC.

We made it to the restaurant an hour later, and were seated shortly near the window. I already knew what I wanted since Olive Garden was one of my go to casual restaurants. I had a side order of mozzarella sticks, and lasagna, and to drink I had a margarita. David ordered the same, except he had iced tea because he was not much of a drinker. This man was making quite an impression so far. After the waiter left, we picked our conversation back up. He told me that although we just met, he liked me, and he would do everything to show me that he was there to stay.

"I can tell that you have been hurt in the past, and I won't make any promises to never hurt you. Instead, I want to show you what my plans are with you." I didn't confirm nor deny his statement, I just listened to him intently like Joanne had advised. "You seem very ambitious for a person your age." I was pursuing my MBA while working full-time. "Dominique, I like you, so I will take things as slowly as you want because I am not going anywhere." Although he seemed sincere, I wasn't really moved because I had to learn the hard way that most men were liars. This was the part that got scary because I didn't trust myself to make good decisions concerning men anymore. I prayed to God that this would not turn out to be another disappointment, and I guess he answered my prayers.

After dinner, he wasn't ready to end the night yet because he was enjoying my company, and asked if I wanted to catch a movie. I wasn't ready to end the night yet either, but didn't express that to him. During the movie, he held my hand, and was such a gentleman.

I could tell he still wasn't ready to go home after the movie, and he suggested we take a short walk. He told me that he had a really nice time, and he hadn't felt this comfortable around a woman in a long time, and he liked the fact that I was easy to be around. He asked when he could see me again. I had to admit that I had a good time as well, and told him we could see each other over the weekend. He said he would surprise me. I didn't really like surprises, but I was willing to go along with it. He hailed a cab for us to ensure I made it home. I lived downtown Brooklyn, and told him that it wasn't necessary, but he insisted.

When we arrived, he told the cab to wait, while he walked me upstairs to my door. He kissed me on the cheek and said good night. It was late, so I opted to call the girls at work the next day. I laid down and thought about the evening, and how much fun I had. I could really see David as a potential, but didn't I see a future with Kenneth as well? That didn't turn out with a happy ending. I wanted to be able to enjoy thoughts of the date without thinking about the future, but I was afraid to open up because I might end up getting hurt again. I know it was out of my control, but those thoughts dominated my mind. Thinking about starting a new relationship was scary. I couldn't think of a relationship without thoughts of Kenneth creeping up on me. The next day at work I called Joanne and Stacey to fill them in on my date with David. I called my friend and thanked her for the introduction and chastised her for not telling me how fine David was.

For our second date, he surprised me with tickets to see Miss Saigon, and afterwards he took me to an upscale restaurant. I really liked his style. It was mature and sophisticated. I was beginning to look at David in a new light. He seemed like a safe person to be with that could give me the security and stability I was looking for. He ordered for me, and I found that very attractive. Once the waitress left, he took my hand in his and told me that he would do whatever it took to make me happy. He said he was not trying to scare me away, but he wanted me to know he wanted to do right by me. What was I supposed to say, he left me speechless, and that was not usual for me. I decided to take a chance by opening up a little to him, and I told him a little about my relationship with Kenneth, and how my relationship with him left me feeling broken and a little insecure. "Instead of telling you, I'll be different, I will let my actions speak for the man that I am. You are it for me." Just like that, he said he knew I was the one he wanted to spend the rest of his life with. When our meals arrived, we ate the tasty dishes and sat there in silence. I didn't really know what to say. David revealed a lot, and it was scary for me because I liked him, and wanted to let him into my life. *Could I trust myself? Should I trust my instincts?* After Kenneth, I began second guessing myself all the time about men which is part of the reason I had not dated after our breakup.

After dinner, we took a nice stroll through the city and talked. Again, he insisted on taking the cab ride home with me. He told the cab driver to wait again, and he walked me upstairs. Before he left, he gave me a kiss on the cheek. I said goodnight and he left. He called me when he got home, and we made plans to spend the following day together. We decided to go to the museum of modern art. After hours at the museum, we had a late lunch. We went to the planetarium at central park, and then we went to the top of the Empire State Building. I felt like a tourist in my own city. I was beginning to feel comfortable with him, so I thought it would be a good idea to invite him over. It's as though we were both avoiding that issue. As we left the Empire State Building, I asked him if he wanted to come over and keep me company for the rest of the evening. I told him we could either watch movies or play games. We took a cab home. I showed him around the apartment, and he was really impressed with it. We settled in the living room and started playing the game "Trouble". After a while we switched to Black Jack. To make it interesting, I thought we should play for money. When I kept winning, I decided to add incentive and play strip Black Jack. At first, I was winning, and all he had left was his pants. All of a sudden, the tides turned and I found myself having to take my clothing off. Now, I was down to my sexy matching Victoria Secret underwear. I thought now was a good time to stop before things went any further.

He took that as his queue and came over to me and started kissing me. David was a great kisser. We kissed for a long time, and he sucked on my tongue and lips. He began kissing my neck and went down until he got to my chest, he unsnapped my bra, and began sucking on each breast one by one to ensure that they both got the attention they deserved. It felt sooooo good to be touched again, and I realized how much I missed this part of my life. He paused and asked me if I wanted him to stop. Although I didn't want him to, I told him yes. I asked him to spend the night. He held me and didn't try anything else. I respected him for that. The next morning, I woke up and made us breakfast. We decided to stay in that Sunday. We watched movies and talked, and I ordered pizza. When he called that night, he wanted to know if this meant that we were exclusive. I said yes.

16

DATING AGAIN

Joanne

HEN I GOT home, I called Dominique and told her about my date with William. She told me everything was going great with her and David, and that if things continued going good with William maybe we should all get together soon, so she could meet him, and I could meet David. She had been dating David for six months now, and although I had spoken to him a few times, I had yet to meet him. We talked for a little while longer and I asked her how school was going and she said she was hanging in there. I decided to call Stacey and tell her about William. Stacey had been going out with the same guy now for two years, they met while in school, and everything seemed to be going well with them. I filled her in and she was happy for me because she was tired of my depression over Bernard, and she was happy that I was going out again because all I did was work and sleep. After I got off the phone, I thought about calling William to tell him I had a good time, but decided against it. I would let him do the calling for now. William called me as I was laying in the bed watching TV, to tell me that he had a good time, and hoped that the next time we had a break in our schedules we could hang out again. I told him that was cool with me.

We didn't get to see each other again until the following week. It was a Friday night after work. He said he wanted to go to dinner. I headed home to get dressed and he came to pick me up. I wore a long navy-blue wrap skirt with a yellow turtleneck with my black leather boots and my black leather coat. I was ready when William arrived and he seemed relieved that he didn't have to wait a long time. We had spoken through the course of the week, so we both felt more comfortable in each other's presence. We went to a restaurant in Park Slope. I looked over the menu and asked for water while I decided on what to eat. This was a very nice restaurant. I lived in Brooklyn all my life and did not know about this restaurant. After we ordered, we began talking. He talked about work for a while and the hectic week at the hospital, and then he started telling me why he decided to become a doctor.

I told him that I basically became a nurse because my mother was a nurse, and it just seemed like what was expected of me, and I never really thought about anything else. He told me about his family. He was part of a big family; he had five brothers and four sisters, and he was somewhere in the middle. I asked him what it was like to grow up with so many siblings, and he said there were times when it was fun and other times it was annoying. He said his parents were working middle class. His dad was a plumber, and his mother had recently started selling desserts, but before that she was a housewife. He said he enjoyed having his mother at home, so if he had his way, he would want to have a housewife as well. I thought that was interesting because you didn't find many men who still felt that way, and if they did some of them would not be able to provide for a family with one income. He said that was another reason he went into the medical field so that he could earn enough money to afford his future wife the opportunity to stay home. I didn't oppose women who stayed home, but I never thought that far ahead concerning myself. I just assumed if I got married and had children, I would go back to work and have a relative or close family friend take care of the child while I went back to work.

That subject led to other interesting topics, and then our food arrived. After dinner, it was still early, so we went to the Billiards to play pool. I was a good pool player, and I showed off my skills and shocked William. Out of the three games we played, I beat him twice. Instead of being a sore loser, he was impressed. We drove to the make out spot at Prospect Park. I called it that because so many other cars were parked and there was nothing but couples around. We reclined our seats, and we talked about our evening. I told him I was actually having a lot of fun hanging out with him, then I got serious and told him about my relationship with Bernard. I didn't tell him all the details because it was too early for all of that, but I told him that I still wasn't completely over it yet. He was silent for a moment, and instead of responding, he reached over and stroked my cheeks, looked into my eyes and leaned over and kissed me softly. Kissing William was nice. We were kissing for a good while when he pulled away. He asked me if I was ready to start something new or did I need more time? I said I was ready to start something new because it was time I moved on with my life. This time I reached over to continue the kiss and didn't stop until his alarm started going off. I leaned on it and triggered it accidentally. We both laughed and took that as a sign to head on home.

I called Dominique, but she wasn't home and neither was Stacey. I took a shower and thought about the evening. William seemed to be nice, he had a bright future, and he was a good kisser. I was excited, and I felt like a schoolgirl that just had her first kiss because it seemed that way. This was my first kiss since the break-up with Bernard. The phone ringing broke me out of my thoughts, and it was William calling me to tell me he made it home. We talked for a bit and said we would try to schedule something as soon as our schedules allowed. I fell asleep with positive thoughts about William.

Dominique called me the next morning, and asked if I was free to hang out. When I arrived at Dominique's, Stacey was already there. Dominique cooked breakfast, and we all dug in. Afterwards, we sat around her kitchen table filling each other in on our recent dating experiences. I told them about my date with William, and how it was simple, and nice to be in a man's company again. Dominique said that she definitely understood that because it wasn't until she met David that she realized the same thing. Her and David had gone on a date to Tavern on the Green in Central Park, and she said it was very nice, then she said afterwards they went back to his place and had a great night.

Stacey usually went to the movies and to eat and then back to her boyfriend's place. They went to other places and all, but she said Friday night became the ritual movie night. Either they would go out to the movies or rent movies, or watch movies on cable. Stacey's boyfriend was the supervisor at Verizon, attractive and seemed like a really cool dude. I asked her if she was happy, and she said she was, but sometimes she wondered if there was someone else out there for her. She wondered if she was settling for him because everything fell into place and she never questioned it. She said she loved him, and was in love with him, but it wasn't with the intensity of what I shared with Bernard, or what Dominique and Kenneth had. I said, "that type of love is wonderful if you experience it, but you shouldn't leave something good to go chasing after it." It seemed like there was always an obstacle that seemed to be in the way of being with the love of your life. We stayed on that topic for a long time and talked about how you knew if someone was the love of your life. Dominique said she knew with the first kiss, and it felt like kissing someone for the first time even though you had obviously kissed other people before. I agreed with her and added that you felt complete in places you never knew felt empty before.

It seemed even if you were lucky enough to experience the love of your life, it was followed by a bitter ending. We couldn't think of anyone we knew that was married to the love of their life. In my case, Bernard was not only the love of my life, he was my first love, my first lover, and the first of so many other things. Dominique said, although Kenneth wasn't her first, he was the first person to touch her physically and emotionally the way he did. She also wondered if she would ever share those experiences with anyone else. "How does David make you feel?" She explained that what she had with David was on a different level because he made her feel safe and secure and didn't doubt his words because his actions and words matched so far.

I guess that was a good way of looking at it. She could definitely see herself marrying David because she trusted him completely, and she didn't think she would ever trust another man after the devastation with Kenneth. She realized she couldn't hold Kenneth's mistakes against David, and David worked hard in earning and keeping her trust. She also learned that there were no guarantees when it came to love and we had to pray for the best outcome. When did she become so wise? Hearing Dominique gave me the hope I needed to know that it was possible to find another relationship that was fulfilling. I thought maybe William could be that person, I would just have to wait and see. Dominique added that another good thing was the fact that sex was great between her and David, and he wasn't afraid to please her in any way. Stacey was satisfied with her relationship in that department as well and tried to keep things exciting for him, so they wouldn't fall into a rut.

We were all thinking about what we would eat for lunch and do for the rest of the day when Dominique's phone rang. We all knew who it was, since we were over at her house. She was all smiles when she greeted David, and it was cute to see her smile genuinely again. He wanted to stop by later, so she told him we were hanging out, but he could stop by later if he liked. He declined stating she should have her girl time and didn't want to interrupt our women bashing session and we all laughed. We decided to order pizza for lunch, and looked over Dominique's movie collection. We picked Set it Off and Jason's Lyrics even though we already saw them both. We each made comments during the movie as if we hadn't seen it plenty of times before. We had a fun girl's day and headed home later in the evening in a good and light mood.

William called me early the next morning and asked me if I wanted to have breakfast before our shifts started. I told him I would meet him at the diner by the hospital. He said he hoped I didn't mind him calling me so early to get together. He couldn't stop thinking about me, and was looking forward to seeing me and didn't know when he would get the chance with both our busy schedules. At that moment, I thought about the fact that we only shared one kiss, and I was looking forward to kissing him again. I was wondering when we would get a few private moments alone so that we could kiss again. Thinking about my lack of privacy at home, I decided I would start looking for an apartment in the spring.

Christmas was approaching and I didn't know whether or not to buy anything for William because we had only been dating for a few weeks. I didn't know the rules on things like this. Besides, I didn't even know what to get him. It would be easier to ask him, but what if he wasn't even thinking about it, and felt that he had to do something because I brought it up. I didn't want him to feel like I expected anything. I never really gave dating this much thought before, Dominique and Stacey were lucky that they didn't have to deal with these issues anymore. The woes of dating in the early stages.

I decided that I would get him something simple because I wanted to. I got him a teddy bear dressed in a doctor's uniform, and a nice X-mas card. On X-mas day, we were both off, so we decided to spend the day with our families, and got together later in the afternoon. I met him at his place. His apartment was small, but neatly organized. He had shelves of medical and science books up against the wall. It seemed like he kept every book from every class he had ever taken. He put the radio on, and an X-mas jingle was playing. He excused himself and came back with a wrapped box, and handed it to me. I handed him his bag and opened my gift. I didn't want to tear the wrapper because it was wrapped so nicely. It was a red hat, scarf, and glove set. I thanked him, and I reached over to kiss him on the cheek, but he turned his face and it landed on his lips instead which led to a long-awaited kiss. When we parted lips, he pulled his teddy bear out of the bag and hugged me. He hadn't received a teddy bear in a long time, but he liked it. We talked a little about the day that was spent with our families and the event that took place then fell into a nervous silence. Nervous because I could tell he wanted to make a move, but wasn't sure if he should or not.

I moved in closer to him, and he started kissing me again. I felt his hands exploring my body. He pulled my sweater off over my head. He started kissing my neck and lowered his head toward my breasts. I missed this feeling, I felt his hands begin reaching down to unzip my pants. That's when I moved his hands, and he stopped and looked at me and asked what was wrong. I told him I wasn't ready to take it there yet. He paused for a minute and started kissing me again. I wrapped my arms around him and he deepened the kiss. I let my hands explore his body, and when I got to his pants, my hands froze. I wanted to touch him, but I didn't want him to think I was leading him on. He sensed my hesitation and led my hand towards his private part. I felt his hardness, and William was impressive. I was on the verge of breaking down and giving in to William when his phone rang. He was going to ignore it, but I told him to go get it. I used that moment to gather myself. I put my bra and sweater back on and sat up waiting for him to come back. When he came back, I could tell he was a bit disappointed, but he didn't say anything.

He came and sat back down next to me. He asked me if I wanted to help him put together a jigsaw puzzle. He got really serious and was really studying the pieces. He looked so cute, I stopped just to stare at him. He didn't notice at first. Finally, he looked up when he realized that I had not been trying to put any pieces together. "I can see you really get into it." He said he could get carried away sometimes. We worked on the puzzle for a bit, and I left before it got too late. He walked me downstairs to my car, and kissed me goodbye.

I called Dominique and we called Stacey on a three-way so we could fill each other in. We talked for a little while longer, and confirmed what time we would get together the next evening. A few minutes after I hung up the phone with them, William called. He had been trying to reach me for a while, but my phone was busy. He said he wanted to apologize for earlier because he didn't want to make it seem like he was rushing me and didn't want to do anything to make me feel uncomfortable. He wanted to know what my plans were for the upcoming weekend. Aside from work, I didn't have any plans, so we set a date.

On Friday, Stacey and I met up at Dominique's house after work. We all sat in the living room and toasted drinks to each other and exchanged gifts. I had gotten Dominique some Chanel perfume, and a gift certificate to Macy's. I had gotten Stacey a gift card to a furniture store. Dominique had gotten me a leather coach bag, and a sweater. Stacey had gotten me a portable cd player and two cd's to go with it. Dominique bought Stacey a comforter set, and a bed sheet set. Stacey got Dominique a watch, and a gift certificate to Macy's also. After our gift exchange we talked and chilled out for the rest of the evening.

On Saturday, I was anxious about seeing William that night. I wore my uniform to work and brought a change of clothes with me. After my shift, William and I met in the lobby area. We walked out together and he told me to follow him in my car. We went to an arcade place in the city. The place was packed. We had a good time playing games. He had a competitive spirit, but so did I. We ate and headed back to his place afterwards since that's where my car was parked.

On New Year's we spent the evening together. We decided to go to Times Square to watch the ball drop. It was crowded and freezing. Right after the ball dropped, we fought our way through the crowd, so that we could head back to his place. He made us some hot chocolate, and we sat in his living room. He told me he really enjoyed going out with me, and he wanted to make us official for the New Year. He said he was looking forward to the New Year with us together as a couple, we toasted to that and sipped our hot chocolates. We sealed the deal with a kiss that lingered. I wanted to stay a while, but I didn't want for us to start anything that I had no intention of finishing. I told him I had to get going, and he walked me downstairs to my car, and gave me another lingering kiss.

William and I spent time together whenever our schedules would allow, and other times we would work something out around our schedules. Everything was going good with William for the most part, although I noticed that he had a real stubborn side to him. If he didn't want to do something there was no way to make him do it, but if he wanted to do something he would expect it to get done. Another thing was the fact that if we disagreed on something, he felt he had to get the last word, and if he didn't like the direction of the conversation, he would walk away from it and didn't want to hear about it again, unless he brought it up.

I didn't really care, so usually when he got like this, I would be the one to mend things. They weren't major things, so it didn't bother me that much. Spring was approaching, and I decided I would use the change in weather to actively look for an apartment. William and I still hadn't slept together yet, and I wanted to change that really soon. I didn't really have privacy at home like that, and his apartment was not the place where I wanted us to share that moment. Looking for an apartment was not the easiest thing, especially since I didn't have much time. I finally found an apartment in Park Slope in a brownstone. Dominique heard about the vacancy through someone she knew, so I was able to move in quickly. Now I would be closer to Dominique's place.

I had some time and decided to use it to go furniture shopping and get settled into my new place. Dominique helped me shop for furniture and home decor. I wanted an off-white Italian leather sofa. I know it wasn't the most practical, but I liked the look. I found a plush off-white rug to match and was excited at how everything would come together. I wanted to get some art for the living room and bedroom, so we went to this black owned store downtown, and I selected the pieces I wanted. Our next stop, I bought a microwave, toaster, blender, pots, pans, and other kitchen utensils. I was spending money faster than I made it. Dominique bought me a few sheet sets, and towels. It's like the more we shopped, the more things I remembered I needed. Afterwards, we went to get some home essentials, that included an ironing board, soap, and other cleaning supplies, so I could clean the apartment before I moved in. I needed to get some blinds for the windows, so we went to Home Depot for that, and while there I picked up other stuff I needed. Moving was a huge expense, and thankfully, I saved all my money while living at home.

When we made it home, we were fatigued, and I didn't even want to think about how much money I spent. I slept at Dominique's place that night since she was closer to my apartment. I called my machine and found that William left three messages. I called him back. We spoke for a bit, and he said he would be available to help with my deliveries. When David called Dominique, the clear expression of love was written all over her face when they spoke. I thought about William, and although I really liked him and spending time with him, I wasn't at that point yet, and I didn't know yet if I would ever be there with him.

The next morning, I headed to the apartment early because the phone/cable company was supposed to arrive between eight-thirty and noon. William got there half an hour after I did. As we waited, I was glad he bought a radio and cards to keep us occupied while we waited. I started to clean the apartment and he helped. He cleaned the bathroom, while I cleaned the kitchen. I was startled when I heard the bell. I didn't expect the cable company to come on the earlier side of the window. When I opened the door, the guy from the phone company was really cute. He was making friendly conversation, and flirting when William came out of the bathroom. He greeted him and the phone guy's demeanor changed immediately. He went about his work, and William just glanced at me and went back to the bathroom. Two hours later, the cable and phone lines were installed. It was time for a food break, so I headed to the deli and bought two hero sandwiches, chips, and soda. We ate, but I noticed William was a little quiet. When he came back to the kitchen, he said, "if I wasn't here would you have taken that guy's number or given him yours?" I said, "why would I give him my number when we're together." He said, "seeing another man flirt with me annoyed him and he didn't want to lose me." He reached over and kissed me.

Throughout the day, I had other deliveries and there was definitely lots of progress made. William stayed until it was time for him to head to the hospital. After William left, I busied myself putting things away. I had a big hall closet where I put the towels. I hung up the shower curtains, and fixed the bathroom up. Dominique and Stacey came over to help out after they were done with work. I was glad they came with pizza. They helped tremendously and promised to return over the weekend to help.

I got home and packed some clothes that would last me through the week. I threw some sexy underwear and sleepwear in there because I wanted to look nice for William for our first time. I took my small TV, since that wouldn't take up too much space. After I was done at home, I stopped by the grocery store to pick up some things to cook, and I also bought some condoms. I wanted to put everything away, and take a quick shower and get comfy before William arrived. After I came out of the shower, I put lotion all over my body, and wore a silk sleep shirt. I was watching TV when the doorbell rang.

I ran downstairs, and greeted him with a kiss at the door. He followed me upstairs where I took his jacket off and hung it on the door. "Are you hungry?"

"No!" I turned the TV off, and led him to our comforter. I sat him down and climbed on top of him and pulled off his shirt. I started kissing him, and he caressed my breasts. He turned me over and was on top of me. He pulled his pants off, and I reached under the pillows for the condom. He smiled, and fingered me for a while to make sure I was nice and ready to receive him and put the condom on. He slid inside me, and he felt good. He started pumping, and grunting, and before I had a chance to catch a rhythm, he was done. I was disappointed. You felt so good to me baby. I couldn't even respond to him. He rolled over to catch his breath, and said I'll be ready for round two in a minute. I turned over and held my back to him, and he reached over to hold me, at that moment I really missed Bernard. When would he stop haunting me? I know you weren't supposed to compare people, but Bernard always took his time to please me. William didn't even go downtown, he said that was something he wanted to do with his wife. I let that slide, but I wanted to be with someone who at least took the time to please me as well. He started rubbing my back and turned me over on my back and gave me a nice back rub.

He started kissing me again and started the process all over again. This time he retrieved the condom from his pants pocket, and slid inside. He lasted longer this time around and tried to satisfy me, but there were no fireworks for me. I thought to myself, would it be shallow to break up with a good guy over something like this? I wanted to be alone, but I couldn't tell him to go home. I could wait it out, maybe sex would get better over time because I liked him. William fell asleep shortly after, I on the other hand was wide awake. When he was asleep for a while, I slid out from under his arms and went to my bedroom to look out the window and think. My thoughts were of Bernard. I cried silently because his memory was still haunting me, and I felt like I wouldn't find what I had with him with anyone else. Then I thought of William. All in all, he was a good guy, but he didn't excite me like Bernard did. I washed my face and went back to the living room. I fell asleep as soon as my head hit the pillow.

In the morning, I made breakfast, and William hung the blinds and other things that needed hanging. I busied myself wiping down the rest of the apartment, while I waited for the furniture delivery. We stopped to eat lunch, and William started talking about how much last night meant to him, and how special I was to him. He said being with me was all that he hoped for. The ring of the doorbell halted our conversation, and I was glad. I didn't want to lie to him about yesterday, and I didn't know how to tell him that he didn't really excite me. When they got all the furniture upstairs, the sofa and loveseat were situated how I wanted them to be. I dozed off a little when I heard the doorbell. William was back from the grocery store and he busied himself in the kitchen making dinner. I dozed off again and William woke me up when the food was ready. He made baked macaroni with ground beef and salad. This was one of the thoughtful things I liked about William. He knew French and

Italian dressing were my favorite, so he got both because I always went back and forth on which to use. The food was good, I ended up having seconds, and there was still some left over.

Dominique and Stacey dropped by later that evening, and this was their first time meeting William. William stepped out for a little bit, so that gave us girls a chance to talk. I told them about the previous night's episode, and they both agreed that he seemed like a cool guy and I should just work on it. William came back in with a handful of roses. They both oohed and aahed, and I wanted to know why mister was showing off in front of my friends. He put the flowers in a vase and kissed my cheek. Dominique and Stacey took that as their cue and left.

He pulled me off the chair and led me to the bathroom. He prepared a bubble bath for me which was quite nice and relaxing. When I was ready to get out, he returned and toweled me dry and rubbed lotion all over my body. He led me to the bed and I relaxed while he went and showered. He came over to the bed and started kissing me, my nipples hardened at the touch of his hands, and he licked them ever so lightly. He slid down to my stomach, and then to my private area. I got excited for a brief second, but was disappointed quickly when he continued to my thighs. He paused and then fingered me and watched my reaction to his touch. I pulled his head up to meet mine, and started kissing him. I reached for a condom and put it on him and he slid inside. I told him to go slowly and he did. He lasted longer than before. It was better this time, but it still wasn't where I wanted it to be, but I would be patient and continue to work on sex with him.

That weekend as planned Dominique, Stacey and their crew helped me move into my apartment. We blasted the music and busied ourselves working. The guys put my mahogany poster bed together for me, and put the dresser and nightstands that went with it where they belonged. As they moved in other stuff I started to unpack some boxes, and hung clothing up in my closet. For lunch we ordered pizza as usual. As the evening wound down, David left with Dominique followed by Stacey and her boyfriend.

William and I fell into a comfortable rhythm. Most of our alone time was spent at my place. We didn't get to spend that much time together because William's residency was ending, and he had to complete his final exams. William accepted an offer to work in a hospital on the upper east side in the city, and I took him out to celebrate the good news. I made reservations at the Rainbow room. The atmosphere was very nice, and we had a great time. He said the first thing on his agenda was to find a decent place to live. He was thinking of staying in the city, but he wasn't sure yet. At dinner, William revealed to me that he was falling in love with me, and I was stunned because I didn't feel the same way, at least not yet. He must have read my mind because he said it was okay if I didn't feel that way, but he knew I would feel that way for him in time. He wanted to let me know how he felt. I squeezed his hand and gave him a warm smile. That night when we got back to my place William made love to me very intensely, and I was hoping this would really be a turning point in our relationship as far as the physical was concerned, but that wasn't the case at all.

William had a very busy schedule at the hospital he was work-ing at, so he didn't find an apartment until early August. He found a place in Harlem that was nice, but a longer commute. I hoped we could continue with the routine of my place. His apartment was good for him because he didn't have a long way to travel when he got off work.

William called me one morning before I went to work, and told me he was coming over after his shift ended at eight, and that he had a nice surprise for me. I was anxious all day at work because I was wondering what this surprise could be. When I got home, I hurriedly started dinner. I made spaghetti with ground beef, and I bought some fresh baked bread. I made some lemonade and waited for William to arrive.

When William arrived, he greeted me with a passionate kiss. "What's the surprise," I asked. I couldn't wait any longer. "Let's eat first. I'm hungry." I was secretly at my wit's end because I really wanted to know what the surprise was. Finally, after eating, he said that he was able to get Labor Day weekend off, so he booked us a quick getaway. I was really excited. He showed me the brochures for the room we would be staying in and it looked remarkable.

We drove up to the Poconos after work on Thursday, and we were tired when we got there, so we showered and went to bed. William woke me up Friday morning with kisses down my back. We decided to take a shower together. William washed my body down then I did his. He picked me up and I wrapped my legs around his waist and he entered me with a nice deep stroke, although sex was better with him, I felt like there was a spark that was missing. Afterwards, William had a nice surprise up his sleeves, he went downtown, and surprisingly he wasn't bad at all, and it made me wonder if he was telling the truth about this being his first time.

After that, I wanted to relax and stay in, but William said we should go out and enjoy the nice weather. We decided to go for a swim and had lunch after. Later, we played a game of volleyball and capped our day off with a delicious dinner. I told William that I was really enjoying myself so far, and I was glad that he planned this mini getaway for us. When we got back to the room, I undressed William. He was surprised when I went downtown on him. Although he didn't ask me to do it, I thought it was only fair since I really enjoyed it earlier in the day. That was also my subtle hint that I wanted him to do it again, and he did. I was very satisfied the second time around, and I was ready to just roll over and go to sleep, but William was not done yet. We fell asleep cuddled into each other with our clothes scattered everywhere.

The rest of the weekend whizzed by, and we had to leave early Monday morning and head back home. On the drive home, I thanked him again for the getaway because it was quite relaxing, and we had a wonderful time. I thought about how much fun I had in such a short weekend, and I marveled at how much more I enjoyed being with William when he went downtown. I noticed that William seemed like he was in a different zone while we were at the Poconos, and I hoped that this was not short lived, and that this would be how things would be from now on.

I didn't have to wait long before I found out. Although the sex was not bad, I realized I enjoyed it more when he went downtown. I didn't feel I should have to ask him to do it because he knew how much I enjoyed it. About a month after our trip, I finally asked him why he hadn't done it since. He said it just wasn't something he really enjoyed doing, so I pointed out to him that he enjoyed it when I gave him head and didn't stop me when I did it. "I give you head because I know you like it and I would just like it if you consider reciprocating it in return because you know how much I like it." He ended the conversation although I felt there was no resolve which was one of the things that got on my nerves about him. If we were discussing something and I didn't want to talk about it anymore, he would keep at it until he got his point made or until he got his way, but with him if you kept at it he would just walk out or hang up, if we were on the phone.

In November, we spent our first Thanksgiving together as a couple. This was my first time meeting his family and I was a little nervous. When I got to his house his father made me feel at home right away, his mother warmed up to me after some time. His family had a large gathering since he had lots of siblings and nieces and nephews. It was nice to meet his family, but I was glad when we headed to my parents' house. My brother's girlfriend was there and they had already eaten. I introduced them to William, and I noticed right away that they weren't as warm to him as they had been to Bernard. As the evening progressed, they got more comfortable with him and my father asked him to join the men for a game of dominoes, and the girls stayed upstairs and talked. We decided to hit the road. Both William and I had to work the next day, so we headed home before it was too late and fell asleep immediately.

After Thanksgiving came the anxiety of Christmas shopping, and I had no idea what to get William. Two weeks before Christmas, I went shopping with Dominique and Stacey. I narrowed it down to two J. Crew sweaters, one was a thick off-white turtleneck and a navy-blue wool sweater, slacks and cologne. I wanted to get Dominique and Stacey's gift, but I didn't want them to see what it would be, so I took note of things they were checking out and came back alone to buy it for them. I bought gifts for my family, and that concluded shopping for everyone else.

Christmas fell on a Thursday that year, and both William and I were working, but we had the early shifts. He came to pick me up from work, so we dropped by his family's house to drop off their gifts, and then to my parents' house. As soon as we got to my house, William pulled me to him and kissed me deeply then said Merry X-mas, and handed me a package. I ripped it open to find an XO chain, bracelet, and ring. He put the chain and bracelet on for me and I slid the ring on my right-hand ring finger. It was beautiful and I was excited about my gift. I went under the tree and got one of his boxes for him to open. It was the Armani cologne set with the aftershave and deodorant. He liked it and thanked me with a kiss. He handed me another box, and I ripped that open to find a nice black evening gown with a card that said we had reservation to Tavern on the Green for New Year's Eve. I couldn't believe it. It was the right size and everything. I excitedly thanked him, and went to get two more boxes for him. He opened the smaller box that had a silver Movado watch inside which I had decided to get him at the last minute. He liked it, and I put it on for him, and he thanked me with another kiss. He opened the other box with his sweaters and slacks, and he approved of the outfits I bought him. Then he handed me a card. It read, *"Joanne I Love You, and I hope our love lasts always. Merry X-Mas. I hope to come home and find you there."* He also had the keys to his apartment in the envelope. I slowly unbuttoned his shirt, and kissed his chest, and then I unbuckled his pants and trailed kisses along his hardness, and took him in my mouth. Everything was intense that night, and William left me feeling quite satisfied. I told him I loved him too. We fell asleep in each other's arms. I fell asleep looking forward to the New Year, which would mark our anniversary.

On Friday Dominique, Stacey, and I did our usual sleepover. I had gotten Dominique an outfit from DKNY that she had her eye on. I had gotten Stacey an outfit from Banana Republic. Dominique got me another Coach bag, and some perfume, and Stacey got me an outfit from A/X. We exchanged the rest of the gifts, and then sat down at the table to eat and talk. Dominique had picked up some Haitian food from a restaurant, and we dug in. We talked about the gifts from our boyfriends, and how we spent our holiday, and about plans for the New Year's. David bought Dominique jewelry, clothes, and a laptop. Stacey's boyfriend bought her clothes, and jewelry. It was nice that we were all in a happy place. We chilled out and listened to music, and talked late into the night. We went for breakfast in the morning, and then parted ways.

When I arrived at William's place, I was about to ring the bell, when I remembered I now had the keys and decided to use it for the first time. William was watching TV in his shorts. He was consumed with a football game and barely acknowledged me. I whipped up something to eat, and brought it to him. I tidied up his place since the game had his full attention. After the game, we headed out and enjoyed ourselves. When we got back to his place, he undressed me and went straight downtown. I was shocked because after our argument in October he hadn't done it, and I hadn't brought it up. I let him please me and thoroughly enjoyed it. New Year's Eve found us together at Tavern on the Green. I wore the dress he bought me, and he wore a black suit, white shirt. When the clock struck midnight, we were at my house deep in a passionate kiss.

In August, William and I took a vacation together to Jamaica. We had a suite that was fully equipped with a living room, kitchen, and dining area. We had a king-sized bed, and our room had a balcony with a view of the beach. William and I had a great time. We shopped, went to the beach, para sailed, jet skied, and any other water sport available at our hotel we tried. Our nights were spectacular. We made love on our balcony, the beach, and in our bedroom. On our last day, I felt so sad because I didn't want to leave. When we returned to NYC, we had a day before we had to return to work, so we relaxed at his place. William had gotten our pictures developed and put them in his album. It was times like this when I appreciated what William and I had and the doubts I had about us would get pushed to the back of my mind. Times like this would make me forget about our arguments and him wanting his way all the time. We looked through the album and reminisced about some of the places the pictures of us were taken.

HERE COMES TROUBLE...

Dominique

MY RELATIONSHIP WITH David was going strong for about a year when we hit a major roadblock by the name of Kenneth. Kenneth contacted me and made his attempt to come back into my life. I came into work one day and found a bouquet of red roses on my desk. I smiled because I thought they were from David, but I read the card a few times to make sure I was seeing correctly. Kenneth apologized for hurting me, and said he was ready to win me back. I guess he thought things would be easy for him like when we first met. I threw the card away, and I called Joanne to tell her about the flowers and some of the old feelings that were stirred up inside of me. I didn't know if I should tell David. What would I say, Kenneth sent flowers and some old feelings were stirred up? I couldn't really concentrate on anything at work that day. I thought about the happy times with Kenneth and all the hurt that he caused me as well. Kenneth was responsible for my trust issues after cheating on me several times throughout our relationship and most importantly having a child with someone else while we were still together.

When I got home that afternoon, Kenneth was standing in front of my door. He looked so good. Hearing his voice again turned me on and I remembered all the things I loved about him. It took me back to the first day we met. I couldn't really hear what he was saying, I was just thinking about being in his arms again, but I couldn't let him see that he still had such a strong effect on me. I didn't want him to know that I still loved him. *Why was he doing this to me?* I had finally moved on with my life, and he chose to show up now. When we broke up I wished that he would call me and tell me that he was sorry for the hurt that he caused me and be the man I wanted him to be. *That call never came, so why now?* I asked him what he was doing here with the sternest voice I could muster. He ignored my question, instead asking if he could come in. I wanted to say no, but I let him in instead. He took a seat and relaxed as though he belonged in my living room. I sat on the sofa across from him and asked again what he was doing here. He avoided my question, and had small talk. I wasn't in the mood to play any games with him, so I sat there quietly and waited for him to speak his mind.

He started by apologizing to me for how things ended. He said he was sorry for the hurt he caused me, and breaking the trust in our relationship. He said he wanted to contact me so many times before, but didn't know what to say because he knew how angry I was, and he didn't think I was ready to forgive him, so he wanted to give me time. "What made you think there would ever be enough time that could pass after the hurt you caused?" He could see I was getting worked up and always had a way of calming me down, and then we would have the best make up sex afterwards. "I know things could never go back to the way they were, but I want to start over." *Was he crazy, it had been two years.* "I know it has been two years, but I am still in love with you and cheating on you was the worst mistake of my life and I know you still love me too." *The audacity of this man.* He said he knew I had a man, but that he wasn't the one for me because he would always be the love of my life. "You are the best thing that ever happened to me, and I have been hurting like crazy since you left me." Before I spoke up, he repeated that hurting me was one of the worst mistakes he had made in his life, and he wanted to make sure that when he came back to me, he had everything in his life together because that's what I deserved. I asked about Jr., and he said he was doing fine. At that moment, I realized that him having a son while we were together still hurt me. Looking at Kenneth, and how my body was reacting confused me. *How was it possible that this man still had this effect on me after all this time?* I secretly wanted to jump in his arms. As quickly as that thought came to my mind, I thought about his betrayal and thought of David.

Thinking about David at that moment made me smile. I was happy David was in my life. I would never love him the way I loved Kenneth, but he gave me stability, and security. For a long time, I thought that Kenneth cheated on me because I didn't do enough or give him enough. I gave him my all but that still wasn't enough, I often blamed myself for his cheating and was very insecure about that. With David, I never felt insecure. He showed me that he appreciated me and the things I did for him. I turned to Kenneth and told him that he was too late. There was a time that I dreamed of this day, and if Kenneth had come back into my life, I would have taken him back no questions asked, fortunately that time had passed.

Although I was not completely over him, and knew he would always have a piece of my heart, I finally moved on. Kenneth would always be the love of my life, but he couldn't have me anymore. I told him that David made me happy and gave me the security that I didn't feel with him. He came over and sat next to me. He told me to look him in the eye and tell him that I didn't love him anymore. He smelled so good and I hesitated before I said, "I love you Kenneth, and I always will, but this is not about how I feel. This is about the fact that I didn't feel secure with you, and I can't ever trust you again. We can't build a family together because you already have one." He touched my face and started kissing me. The kiss sparked up a lot of old feelings, it said all the things that were not said. My mind was telling me to push him away, but my body was responding to Kenneth, like only he could make it. He unbuttoned my blouse, took off my bra, and began to suck on my breasts. My body felt like it was on fire. I wanted Kenneth at that moment. I unbuckled his pants and he unzipped my skirt. In a moment, Kenneth was in me and I felt whole. The sex was intense like old times, and it was out of this world, but I knew then that it was good bye. As intense as this experience was, I realized that I had changed. I could never be with Kenneth again, and I was happy with my current relationship.

Forgiving someone for cheating was possible, but how many times was too many? Kenneth was staring at me with love and admiration as we lay there on the living room floor, and I told him that this was goodbye. I told him that us being together made me realize that although he caused my heart and body to stir, he was a part of my past. He said that he would not give up because he loved me too much, and I told him if he loved me that much, he would let me go and be happy. He asked me If I was going to tell David about what happened. "That is between David and I." That was my polite way of telling him it was none of his business what I would or wouldn't tell David. He said, me leaving him caused him to mature a lot and reflect on his flaws as a man because he realized how much he hurt me and that he messed up the best relationship he ever had, and that I would always have his heart.

I understood what he meant about me having his heart, as he would always have a piece of mine. We lingered a moment longer, and Kenneth kissed me again before he left. I didn't know if that would be the last time I would see him or hear from him, but I knew that chapter of my life was finally closed. I laid there and thought about the fact that although we still had love for each other, we were not meant to be. I used to think that with love you could handle anything, but I now realized that love did not conquer all. I was confused because what ifs were going through my mind. *What if he came back earlier? If I wasn't with David, would I have taken him back? What if David couldn't forgive me? What if he came back again, would this happen again? Wasn't I being a hypocrite, I was heartbroken about being cheated on and I cheated on David with Kenneth of all people.* The ring of the phone brought me out of my thoughts. I wasn't near the caller id, and I didn't feel like talking to anyone anyway, so I let the answering machine pick it up. It was David. His voice was comforting, but I couldn't face him yet. I needed to be alone with my thoughts. That night I slept on the living room floor. The next morning I called out from work because although I could officially say the Kenneth chapter was closed, I was tormented about hurting David in the process. I needed to be alone.

The reality of the situation was sinking in. I cheated on David, one of the things that I was not able to forgive nor forget that Kenneth did to me. A part of me was still in love with Kenneth, and although he came back like I thought I had been waiting for,

I realized I could not and did not want to be with him. The realization that I had a good man sank in, and the fact that he loved me deeply and would not hurt me, but yet I had hurt him. *Was I wrong to choose the man that I cared and loved and felt secure with over the man that was the love of my life, but hurt me badly? Couldn't I get over that hurt?* I thought about calling Kenneth and telling him that I made a mistake and that I was willing to work things out, but the truth was no matter how I felt about Kenneth, he broke something in me and I could never go back. I wanted to call David, so he could comfort me and tell me that everything would be okay, but I couldn't call him expecting that. I thought and thought until I couldn't think anymore. I decided to go for a walk outside, since it was a beautiful day. I took a walk to DUMBO because being by the water usually relaxed me.

It was painful, but saying goodbye to Kenneth was the right thing to do, and gave me the peace I needed to finally move on from him once and for all. I didn't have any lingering thoughts or doubts anymore. Being with him again made me realize that David was the right man for me. I also knew that I had to tell David because I couldn't live with that lie and the guilt would eat me up. I would find out if he was really willing to do anything in order to be with me because staying with me would require a lot of forgiveness on his part. I hoped that we could move past this. If he wasn't able to move past this, I would be devastated, but I would understand. Still, I wouldn't give up without a fight because David was definitely worth fighting for. I continued to walk and I felt a little lighter with each step. I stopped and looked at the water for a while. It really was calming. I walked back home, and felt better. I grabbed something to eat on my way home. When I got back home there were two messages from David. He said he had called my job and I wasn't there, and I wasn't home either. He knew something was wrong and he was worried. I didn't want to talk to David just yet, but I knew I couldn't avoid it any longer.

It had been two days since we had spoken which was not normal for us. David had remained consistent and we spoke daily. I relaxed a bit and debated about whether to call him or not when the doorbell rang. I knew it was him. I let him in, and didn't kiss him like I usually did. He followed me and sat on the couch. I sat next to him, and he immediately knew something was wrong, and waited for me to start talking.

I didn't know where to begin. We sat there quietly for a few minutes, but it seemed like hours had passed because the air was thick and we had never been awkward with each other. Before I could say anything, I got choked up and tears started to fall down my cheeks. He came closer to me, and wiped my tears away. He hugged me and I pushed him away. I would not be able to get it out with him so close to me. I told him that Kenneth sent flowers to my job and was waiting outside my door when I got home two days ago. I paused to see if he was going to say anything or to see if his facial expression had changed. He kept quiet waiting for me to go on. I told him that I realized that Kenneth and I couldn't be together. I paused for a bit before I dropped the final bomb that I had slept with Kenneth.

THE SHOE'S ON THE OTHER FOOT NOW

Dominique

I KNEW THAT WAS a lot of information to process at one time. He sat there in silence, and I didn't know which was worse, his silence or if he would've yelled at me. He finally spoke up and said, "What do you want?" I said, "I want to be with you." He asked me if I was sure. I said, "it's over for Kenneth and I and that was our final goodbye, I love you and I want to be with you." I told him Kenneth was my past and that he was my future. I asked him what he wanted to do. He said that I hurt him and he needed time to think. With that he left. I didn't know what to think. I sat there crying because I didn't know what he would decide.

I didn't hear from David for one whole month. I called and left messages and he didn't respond to any of them which drove me crazy. *I was beside myself. What if he never spoke to me again?* I loved him and didn't want to lose him. Although I was a willing participant, I hated Kenneth all over again. *Why did he have to disrupt my life? Why did I allow him? Why did he still have an effect on me? What if David couldn't forgive me?* I was about to lose my mind. I didn't even want to tell Joanne or Stacey about this because they would probably curse me out and tell me how stupid I was. As if I needed anyone to tell me. I was caught up in the moment of seeing Kenneth, but immediately after I knew I wanted to be with David.

At the end of the first week, when I still hadn't heard from David, I called Joanne and Stacey to come over. I told them what took place. After the shock, they asked me how I was coping with everything. They were so supportive and what I needed. I cried and they took turns comforting me. They said I had to respect David and give him time. They told me to stop calling, and leaving messages. I took their advice and tried to busy myself with work, but I was not in a good place. The pain I felt was even worse than my breakup with Kenneth because I was at fault, and if I lost David, I had no one to blame but myself.

David was a strong man. Exactly one month later, I found him waiting for me in the lobby. He asked me to go for a walk with him. He was silent for a long while before he spoke.

"How do I know that this won't happen again if he comes back into your life unexpectedly?"

I promised him that it was a mistake and that I truly got the closure I needed because I didn't feel the same way anymore which was partially true. In that moment, Kenneth felt like he was a lifetime ago, and part of my past, and he was no longer the person I wanted to marry. I didn't say that to David, but that was the thought running through my mind in that instant. I asked him what I could do, so that he would know that I was truly sorry. He was silent again. "Are you sure about me?"

"YES!"

"I thought long and hard and can't see my life without you and am willing to forgive you. If you ever mess up again, you will lose me for good Dominique and you will regret it." I was so happy that he was willing to forgive me, and I knew I made the right choice when I told Kenneth goodbye. I was lucky to find a good man that made loving him easy and worthwhile. I realized loving Kenneth was one of the hardest things I experienced in my life, and letting go of that love was even more difficult, but the peace of loving David made losing Kenneth worth the heartbreak I felt. I respected and loved David more than I thought possible at that moment. I knew he was where I was supposed to be. Kenneth may have been the love of my life, but at that moment, I knew David was my soul mate.

Making it to the second year of our relationship took a lot of work because we had gone through a rough patch after cheating on him. Things were a little strained in the bedroom at times. The thought that I was with someone else really hurt him. I knew how that felt, so I knew I had to be patient and ride this storm out. After Kenneth cheated, it was imagining him with another woman that got the best of me. I kept picturing that everything he did to me he did it to someone else too. It is hard to go back to normal, after someone you love cheats, so I understood the betrayal David felt. You know your partner had people before you, but the thought of your partner being intimate with another person during the course of your relationship is painful and tortures your mind. I honestly felt that David forgave me because he truly loved me and wanted a future with me. I was angry and disappointed in myself. I hurt David and I knew what that pain was like. It was something I had to endure and work through as well.

There were times when I wanted to call it quits because it seemed like David had not forgiven me yet. I knew all of this was my fault, but I couldn't help but feel that if he decided to stay, he had to truly forgive me so we could move forward. There were times when I wondered if David stayed with me because he wanted to make sure I didn't go back to Kenneth. In the end, we made it through the storm of my infidelity and our relationship was stronger than before.

FOREVER LOVE

OUR THIRD YEAR together David proposed. The crazy thing is that I always thought Kenneth would be the man I married, but marrying David was the best decision I ever made. For our three-year anniversary, he told me to take the day off from work and not to ask any questions and he would pick me up first thing in the morning. David took me on a helicopter ride over the city and that was something I always wanted to do, so I was already pleased with the beginning of our date. Afterwards, we went to the Poconos and he checked us into a really nice suite.

David thought of everything. My bag was already packed and I was wondering how long he had been planning this date. When we entered the room, it was covered in rose petals and candles and there was a huge champagne glass tub in the middle of the floor. He barely closed the door, when I started kissing him and undressed him. I pushed him down on the bed and took him into my mouth. He was very turned on. I got on top and rode him with such an intensity that surprised him. We were both in awe of our session afterwards. We lay there for a bit and then he started kissing me and my neck and my breast. David kissed and licked every part of my body with such fervency that it felt like all the passion he felt for me had been released that day. I came so much that I was a little embarrassed. When he slid inside me, I felt like the room was spinning. Just when I thought we were at a standstill, David showed me that he missed me and loved me. I felt everything he gave that day with everything in my soul.

Our lovemaking suffered while we worked through me being unfaithful, but at that moment, I felt that he had truly forgiven me. There was something different about our lovemaking that afternoon, it felt surreal and like our love had been renewed. We laid there in silence for a while, and he ordered room service for us because we were too tired to go out and eat, and after lunch we fell asleep. When I woke up, I found David getting dressed. He was wearing a suit and had a black cocktail dress out for me to wear. It was a simple dress, but it was exquisite, and I wondered if David had help picking this dress out for me. He gave me a pair of diamond earrings that were beautiful, and I didn't even have David's gift with me because I had been whisked away. I showered and dressed and we headed out to dinner. For a weekday, I was surprised by the number of couples in the dining room.

After a wonderful dinner, we went back to the room, and I got in the tub. I was wondering what was taking David so long when he appeared and got on one knee in front of me. "Dominique, you know I love you." I was already crying. "We have been through a lot, but you make me happy." I felt terrible because I was the cause of our rough patch and the tears flowed heavily and I was fully sobbing. "I can't see my life without you, so I wanted to know if you will be my wife."

"YES!" He put a three-carat princess cut diamond ring on my finger with diamonds around the band that made the ring four carats. It was a gorgeous, sparkling diamond ring. I don't even remember getting out of the hot tub, but I had to thank my fiancé properly.

Meeting David was a blessing for me. I don't know if I would ever completely be over Kenneth, but thoughts of him no longer consumed me or dominated my mind. I realized that what we had was special, but now it seemed like a lifetime ago. I finally knew what true love was and felt like because David showed me what loving someone was really about. David gave me the security and stability that I was looking for. To top it all off, he gave me forgiveness when I didn't deserve it and kept his word of his actions matching his words. He was not the man that I longed for, but he made my heart skip in a way that Kenneth never would or could. He was the man that gave me the calm I didn't know I was looking for. I loved David deeply, but it wasn't with the same intensity of what I felt for Kenneth. However, I understood the difference. Loving David was the kind of love that would last a lifetime. David was tender and attentive to my needs. He showed and expressed his feelings for me and I never felt like I wasn't enough. With David, I wasn't worried about him cheating and trusted him completely. He was patient with me, and included me in his life. He knew I was skeptical to trust and be with someone again.

Being with David was refreshing, and easy. David was very caring, and showed me in every way that he loved me. I didn't doubt how he felt for me. David was considerate to my needs. David showed me that love didn't have to hurt. David and I experienced some tough times, but we managed to find our way back to each other. I couldn't emphasize this point enough. Most importantly, David was forgiving, and it was because of his forgiveness that we had made it this far.

COMMUNICATION IS KEY!

Joanne

ILLIAM AND I got into an argument about a month before Dominique's wedding. He slammed the door to my place and walked out like he usually did in the middle of an argument, but this time I was over it. Here we were engaged talking about a possible wedding date for next year and we couldn't even communicate effectively. *Who was I kidding?* If I admitted the truth to myself, I would also admit that I said yes to William's proposal because he was a decent man, and the fact that he was a doctor didn't hurt either. I loved William, but I think it was only because we had been together for three years now and it happened over time. It wasn't the type of love that was enough to make a lifetime with someone, and I decided that I would tell him that as soon as he called me when he cooled down. I would usually wait a few hours and call him and sometimes apologize to him even though I was right or sometimes he would send me flowers and say sorry, but this time I wouldn't bend. He would have to call me or else we wouldn't speak.

That's exactly what happened too, he didn't call, so we didn't speak. As the days to Dominique's wedding were approaching, I still hadn't heard from him, and for the first time I realized that I didn't care. I should have broken up with William a long time ago, but fear of being alone and not finding someone else kept me in this relationship. I kept telling myself it wasn't all that bad, and most times it wasn't, but William was not the one. I just didn't want to admit it.

On the day of Dominique's wedding, I still hadn't heard from him, and he was my date for the wedding. I let the realization of it all sink in. I mean a month ago, we were talking about getting married, and I was thinking that I would be next, but I guess that was not meant to be. William always told me how much he loved me, and how special I was to him, yet all this time passed with not one word from him. Men! I couldn't figure them out. I laid in bed and a wave of sadness washed over me. I was used to being with William for so long that it felt weird that I would be alone now. I looked at the pear-shaped platinum diamond ring on my ring finger and cried because it seemed happily ever after was not meant for me. First Bernard, and now William. William filled a void in my life, and now I felt empty. I tried not to let these thoughts take over my mind, but I couldn't focus on anything else.

Dominique called me and sounded excited as she asked me if I was up and headed to the hall to start getting ready for her big day. Her cheeriness perked me up a bit. I could tell she wanted to ask about William, but didn't want to bring it up, so I said he still hasn't called me. "Well, it's his loss." I know friends say these things to cheer you up, but sometimes it doesn't help. I changed the subject and asked if she had spoken to Stacey. She said Stacey was already up. When I hung up the phone, I almost called William to ask if he was still coming to the wedding. I was on the sixth digit of his number when I hung up, got up and headed to the bathroom. I stayed in the shower and washed away the thoughts that were running through my mind. When I got out of the shower, I felt more relaxed. I double-checked the bags to make sure that I had packed everything that we would need, and left.

Dominique was ready when I got to her house. She hopped in and we headed to Long Island. We were there in about an hour. When we got there Dominique's hair stylist and make-up artists were already there. She started on Dominique's hair, and I went outside to see how things were coming along. As I went to the reception hall the DJ was arriving to set things up. Everything was going smoothly. As I headed back to our room, I found Stacey there.

THE MOMENT HAS ARRIVED...

Dominique

VERYTHING WAS IN *place so that my wedding day would go smoothly.* There was an orchestra playing, and the ceremony began. There were six bridesmaids in champagne dresses and groomsmen wore navy blue suits with white shirts and gray ties. Joanne was the maid of honor. She wore a strapless dress that was a darker shade of champagne and walked in alone. David's brother, one of the best men, met her half way, and they walked to the altar together. Stacey, the other maid of honor, wore an off the shoulder strapless dress with a split, and she walked down the aisle. David's best friend Anthony, the other best man, met her down the aisle and walked to the altar. After they walked down the aisle, the ushers rolled down the white runner, and the two flower girls dressed in off white dresses walked down the aisle and threw down white roses.

The orchestra played "Here Comes the Bride", and everyone stood. As the doors opened, I was standing there in a beautiful white gown. It was strapless and the top was body fitting with a full skirt. I took my first step to becoming David's wife. As I walked down the aisle, I noticed Kenneth standing there looking at me. *What was he doing here? Was he trying to ruin my day?* He stood in the front looking as sharp as ever wearing a gray pinstripe suit. I couldn't tell what was going through his mind because I couldn't read the expression on his face. I tried to concentrate and just focus on David and how good he looked in his tuxedo smiling at me. As David started walking towards us, I kept my eyes on Kenneth, and he smiled and mouthed I love you. I'm sure no one noticed, but I did, and I was beginning to feel a little nervous. When David reached us, he hugged my dad and took hold of my hand. He whispered I love you, and it felt right. The reason why I was marrying this man came back to me, and although Kenneth was there, his presence no longer disturbed me. I walked down the aisle with David feeling a sense of peace wash over me, and I felt secure and safe.

When we said our vows to each other, I knew I had made the right decision, and this was where I was supposed to be. I knew at that moment that everything would be okay. I was marrying someone who truly loved me and who I truly loved in return. The love I had for David was better than any other love because it was kind, gentle, forgiving, patient, and peaceful. I knew we would make it. At that moment, the love I had for Kenneth almost seemed like it never happened. I was so happy knowing I was David's wife.

MY BEST FRIEND'S WEDDING...

Joanne

AT THE RECEPTION, I danced with one of the best men, Anthony, who was David's best friend. He noticed I wasn't with William, and he wanted to know if something was wrong. I told him William and I had broken up. He said he didn't want to say sorry because that wouldn't be sincere on his part. He expressed that he'd been interested in me for the longest, but David told him I was with William. He asked if it was completely over with William and I said yes. Right then and there he asked me out on a date. I rested my head on his shoulders and was enjoying the dance with him, when I heard someone say can I cut in, and we both looked up to find William standing there. Anthony looked at me to let him know whether or not I wanted to, and I spoke up and said I would talk to him later. He walked back to the table and looked back at me. William spoke first, "I thought I might find you here."

"Was that supposed to be funny?"

William straightened up, "sorry, I didn't think that this silliness would have gone on for so long." He sighed, " I came in person to put a stop to all of it." He continued, "we have to stop these games. I am getting tired of them." I let him say all he had to say. Then I finally spoke up and said, "William! IT'S OVER!" Just two words summed up our relationship. He didn't think I was serious.

"What do I have to do to make it up to you? J, I knew you would be upset, but not this much where you would say such a thing." I told him not speaking made me realize we should have ended things long before. He stepped back and looked at the serious expression on my face. "I know you'll be back, so I will give you your space," and walked away.

I walked back to the table and saw Anthony sitting by himself, and I decided to join him. "Do you want to talk about it?" I said the William chapter of my life was officially over. "I look forward to going out with you soon." We continued to talk. Anthony and I had met on a few occasions at David's events that he attended, we never spoke much maybe because I was with William. All I knew was that he was in the education field.

Anthony was thirty-two years old, and a high school principal. He and David had been friends since childhood. He was happy that David had found himself a good woman. I agreed because Dominique was lucky to have found David. I got lost in my own thoughts, and heard him saying that he hoped to find that one day while smiling at me. I took that time to really look at Anthony. Anthony was very handsome. He was dark-skin, and his hair was cut in a low fade. Maybe I never paid him any mind because I was always with William when I saw Anthony, but staring at him now, he was an attractive guy. He was 6 feet tall, with luscious lips and a beautiful dark complexion. He had a nice body and looked very good in his suit, and the cologne he wore was amazing.

We got up and danced some more, and I really enjoyed his company.

Later in the evening, Dominique came back dressed in an off-white mini dress and got everyone's attention, and said a special thank you to everyone at the wedding, and thanked all her family, and guests for making this day very special and memorable for her. Anthony and I went to wish the happy couple best wishes as they were about to leave for their two-week honeymoon to Hawaii. I gave Anthony a ride home because it turns out, he lived about twenty minutes from me.

When I dropped him off, he said he was enjoying my company and invited me up to his house. He owned the brownstone, and lived on the top level and rented the downstairs. He gave me a tour of his house and I was really impressed with what I saw. We retired in the den which was also his entertainment room. He had a huge TV with surround sound. He asked me what I wanted to listen to. He had an expansive cd collection. I chose a Mariah Carey cd. I settled back on his leather loveseat and he sat in his recliner. We talked into the night about various things and we had a lot in common.

Sometimes, I would say something and he would finish my thoughts. The sun came up on Sunday morning and still found us in his den talking. We both laughed. We decided to have breakfast at the diner by his house. Breakfast was enjoyable, and I liked the company I was in. I could see that this would be the beginning of a new and wonderful friendship. When I got home, I climbed into bed and fell asleep with a hint of a smile on my lips.

EPILOGUE

Dominique

THE PHONE RANG, and it was Joanne calling me to confirm if Madison was ready. She was taking Madison, her god-daughter for the weekend so David and I could celebrate our three-year anniversary. Madison was a happy one-year-old baby that was the light of our lives. Madison was a lucky baby because she was the center of so many people's lives. I smiled as I thought about our anniversary celebration and how lucky I was to have a wonderful husband and a beautiful baby girl.

For our anniversary we decided to go to the Olive Garden because that was where it all began for us. Afterwards, we took in a Broadway show, and stayed at a hotel in the city for the weekend. We thought about going away which wouldn't have been a problem for Joanne, but we didn't want to be that far away from Madison. At the hotel, David gave me two-carat diamond earrings. My gift to him was a gold Movado watch with our anniversary engraved on the inside. We lifted our champagne glasses, to many more years to come.

Joanne

NTHONY AND I were happily married newlyweds. We had been married for one year, and we looked forward to watching Madison because it would give us practice for when we decided to have our own children. Anthony turned out to be my soul mate. He made me realize that Bernard was a significant part of my past, but he was my future. He knew what he wanted and didn't hesitate to go after it. We had been dating for one year when he proposed. He also planned our surprise wedding in Barbados and took care of every detail. Anthony was truly the man I had been waiting for. He showed me how much he loved me every chance he got. Bernard seemed like a distant memory, but I guess there was always a piece of me that would always have a place for him in my heart.

Anthony had my heart because he was my forever. With him I felt peace and security which I never truly had with Bernard. I couldn't change the past, but I could look into my husband's handsome face and see my future and look forward to the life we would share together. We had a great weekend with baby Madison, and I realized it was time to start working on our own little family. Anthony was a great lover, so I would enjoy every minute of trying to have a baby.

AUTHOR'S BIOGRAPHY

E. MICHELLE IS a Brooklyn-based educator with deep-rooted connections to both her home city and her Haitian heritage. Fueled by a fervor for reading and writing, E. Michelle champions the inclusion of Caribbean voices in literature, aspiring to create a world where diverse narratives flourish. Her e-book, "Thoughts of a Black Woman," encapsulates personal reflections that resonate with many, showcasing her commitment to uplifting Black women's experiences through storytelling.

Messages can be sent on Instagram to *@thecollectivecache* or you can check out her blogs at the *www.thecollectivecache.com.*